WORRY

WORRY

A NOVEL

JESSICA WESTHEAD

HARPER **PERENNIAL**

Published by Harper Perennial, an imprint of HarperCollins Publishers Ltd

First edition

HarperCollins Publishers Ltd
Bay Adelaide Centre, East Tower
22 Adelaide Street West, 41st Floor
Toronto, Ontario, Canada
M5H 4E3

www.harpercollins.ca

The author gratefully acknowledges the support of the Recommender Grants
for Writers program, administered by the Ontario Arts Council.

ONTARIO ARTS COUNCIL
CONSEIL DES ARTS DE L'ONTARIO
an Ontario government agency
un organisme du gouvernement de l'Ontario

Library and Archives Canada Cataloguing in Publication
information is available upon request.

ISBN 978-1-4434-5885-6

Printed and bound in the United States of America
LSC/H 9 8 7 6 5 4 3 2 1

This book is for Derek and Luisa, as always,
because they're my people.
But it's also for our friends, because without them,
we would be lost.

ONE

THE MOTHER CAN SEE THE HEART BEATING.

The ultrasound technician points it out to her and the father. Taps the screen with her long, red fingernail. "Here," she says. "Look."

After eight weeks and all the anticipation, the baby is only a small, white blob in a big, black hole. It doesn't look like a person yet.

The father takes a breath and leans closer to the pulsing light and dark. "Hello," he says.

The mother looks away and shakes her head, hard. "No."

The technician and the father turn to frown at her with faces painted in blue and grey. Their expressions say, *Why are you so rudely interrupting our quiet moment of wonder?*

"That's not why we came here," says the mother. "Something's wrong and you're supposed to tell us why."

"Actually," says the technician, "I'm not supposed to tell you anything." She sets down her wand and clicks across the examining-room floor on her precarious heels. They are white and glossy, and their height makes her unsteady until she wobbles to a stop at her desk. The mother had initially seen those shoes and thought, *Really?*

The technician consults the mother's chart. "Oh." She glances back at the screen, which is empty now.

The mother feels tears starting but she will not let them come. Because she is angry. She says, "Look."

Now the technician and the father see what she's showing them.

The long, plastic wand on the table with its giant condom stretched tight, slick with blood. Fresh and bright red in some spots and dark brown and clumped in others. Which the technician must have already seen, because she's the one who put it in and pulled it out.

The mother thinks that right now, in here, *wand* is a ridiculous word. It calls to mind a sparkly fairy flitting around, bestowing happiness. Working magic.

Before they got started, the mother had asked the technician if she could please have the over-the-belly ultrasound instead of the up-the-vagina kind, but the technician shook her head. "It's too early," she said. "We won't be able to see anything that way."

That way would have been so much better, the mother thinks now.

The father says, "But the heart is beating. I saw it, right here." His finger caresses the screen. "That's got to be a good sign, right?"

The technician makes some notes and closes the mother's file. "Not necessarily, no."

His arm falls. "But you showed us."

"I'm sorry."

The mother is lying on her back on the examining table and she feels the trickle between her legs beginning to flow faster. "I need something."

The father is still staring at the screen like he's trying to solve a puzzle.

"Something absorbent. You need to help me with the mess, I'm bleeding more."

"Yes," says the technician. "Just a minute."

While the mother waits, she tries to pretend she's somewhere better, like a beach. The fluorescent sun is beating down and she's lying on the silly towel the father gave her after she giddily unveiled the positive pregnancy test. The towel is bright yellow with red lobsters all over it, and they're wearing T-shirts. And she's soaking it through.

The technician grabs a wad of exam-table paper and thrusts it at the mother. The paper is stiff and scratches her bare skin, but it does the job.

The husband is crying now, very softly.

The wife stares at the ceiling tiles and imagines rising in the air with enormous, leathery wings, being made all-powerful by her hatred for this insensitive, thoughtless person who is supposed to be professional and who is not supposed to show them the heartbeat of the baby that the wife is now in the process of losing.

She will rain down punishment on her for this unforgivable thing, for putting the image of that tiny, useless heart in both of their brains forever.

3

TWO

HERE SHE IS, ALONE BY THE WATER WITH HER ONLY child. It's the middle of the day and the sun is very bright.

Her daughter is lying on her towel on the sand beside her. If she wants to, she can reach out and grab a small, smooth foot, skim her fingers across the slippery material of the pink-and-purple bathing suit with the cartoon pony on the front.

She could do that and reassure herself that her little girl is okay, she's right here. She's where she is supposed to be.

But what happens when she takes her hand away and closes her eyes? Her child disappears. It's that easy. One minute her daughter is there, smiling on the beach on a beautiful summer day. And then she's gone.

Sweat rolls down Ruth's back, and Fern asks her, "What's wrong, Mommy?"

"Nothing's wrong, honey." Ruth squints at the diamonds of sunlight spiking off the lake. "We're just waiting for our friends."

Far above them at the top of a steep set of uneven wooden steps, the enormous A-frame cottage is locked, and Ruth doesn't have a key.

When they arrived over an hour ago, she parked their little hatchback in the driveway next to Stef and Sammy's shiny SUV, got out and freed Fern from her car seat, and then the two of them knocked on the front door, but there was no answer.

It was hot and muggy and Fern wanted to put on her bathing suit immediately. She started to take off her clothes in the front yard but Ruth made her change in the car. She stood guard while Fern shed her top and bottom and wrestled into her suit, her dimpled elbows pinwheeling behind the bird-shit-streaked windows.

The heat was oppressive and Ruth had thought, *It's hotter here than at home. Isn't it supposed to be a few degrees cooler up north?* She fidgeted and wiped her brow.

The cottage loomed over them, surrounded by forest so dense it was dark even in the daytime. The trees huddled together around the property, jagged branches pointing accusations at the expensive piece of land that somebody had hacked out in the centre of them.

The eerie quiet was punctuated here and there by the busy, shuffling sounds Fern was making inside the car as she finished changing. The occasional bird call or random rustling noise was muted, as if the woods had swallowed up every living thing.

There was no sign of any neighbours on either side. Ruth tried to think if she'd seen any other cottages on the long, winding dirt road she'd taken here from the highway. She was pretty sure she hadn't.

Now she sits on the little beach by the dock, perspiring in her tank top and jeans and squinting in the sun because she forgot her sunglasses at home.

She tells her impatient daughter that it's not time for swimming yet.

They can swim when their friends get here.

Although she doesn't know when that will be because

6

Stef isn't answering her phone. She must be somewhere out of range.

But why isn't she here?

Ruth has had to pee for about half an hour now. Her bladder aches.

Maybe she got the address wrong. Maybe Stef and Sammy and the girls are waiting somewhere else, wondering what's keeping them.

Their car is in the driveway, though. *So where are they?*

And then he appears.

A tall man with broad shoulders and black hair, gliding toward Ruth and Fern in nothing but a pair of sunglasses and palm-tree-patterned surf shorts. His paddleboard is nearly invisible beneath the sparkling waves, so it almost looks like he's walking on water. Almost.

He lifts his oar in greeting and calls out, "Ahoy!"

"Ahoy!" Fern calls back, even though she has no idea who the man is.

How many times has Ruth told her to never talk to strangers? Not enough, apparently.

He floats closer and grows larger, cutting through the lake until he reaches the shore. Then he hops off his board and walks right over to them.

"My name's Marvin," he says. "You look lost."

Like they'd washed up on a deserted island with no hope of rescue. Which is actually sort of true. No, it's not. They're fine. They're on vacation!

Ruth shields her eyes, peering at her tiny reflection in the man's mirrored aviators. A halo of sun glows around his silhouette.

"I'm Fern," says Fern.

Ruth sighs and waits for her daughter to ask him for some candy next.

Marvin bows. "It's a pleasure to make your acquaintance, Miss Fern."

Ruth stands up and steps in front of her child's delicate limbs—so much of her soft body exposed to the air. Sticks out her hand, which is shaking but just a little. "I'm Ruth. We're visiting my friend Stef. But this is our first time here so I'm not sure we're in the right place."

"You surely are." His hand is warm when he grasps hers. "Stef's in the lake."

"I'm sorry?" She tries to pull away but he holds on, and she imagines long strands of blonde hair like seaweed, drifting.

"They went for a boat ride. I passed them on my way over here." He releases her.

"Oh." Her arm drops and dangles by her side. "Maybe she forgot we were coming."

"No, she knows. She said to tell you to sit tight and they'll be here soon. How long have you been waiting?"

Fern crosses her arms and frowns. "A million years!"

Marvin's rumbling laugh bounces between the three of them.

Ruth shushes Fern. "Not too long."

"I told Stef she was being a bad host," he says. "If you were visiting *my* cottage, my wife would've served you twelve different types of pie already."

"Pie is squishy inside," says Fern. "Daddy likes it but I hate it."

"Me too." He winks at Fern over his glasses. "Where's your daddy now?"

"He'll be here soon," Ruth says, too quickly.

"He's at our big, new house!" Fern jumps up and down. "We

were in a little house before but Auntie Stef gave Daddy lots of money to buy a new house and now she's our neighbour!"

"She's my neighbour too. Look how much we have in common," says Marvin. "She never gave me any money, though." He puts on an exaggerated pout.

Fern chortles at that, and Ruth tells her, "Auntie Stef didn't *give* Daddy the money, sweetie. Daddy earned it because he works for Auntie Stef. You know that."

Marvin gives Fern a fake-serious look. "And I'll bet he works very, very hard."

There's a splash by the dock, and Ruth turns just in time to see the flash of silver and brown. A big fish, bigger than she'd expect to see so close to shore, leaping up to catch a dragonfly. She even thinks she can hear the jaws snap, but that must be her imagination.

"Your wife sounds like a nice person," she says. "With the pie."

"Yeah," says Marvin. "She's all right."

"Mommy has to go pee!" Fern shouts.

"Shh, Fern." Ruth's face reddens. "No, I don't."

"Yes, you do!" Her daughter jabs a tiny finger at her. "You *told* me you did!"

"I can keep an eye on your little one if you want to scamper into the woods," he says. "I'd let you into the cottage if I could, but I don't have a key. Stef and Sammy trust us with their children, apparently, but not their valuables."

She measures the pain in her bladder against the short distance to the trees and the time it would take to find a secluded spot, pull down her pants, relieve herself, pull them up again and run back.

Marvin smiles at Fern again and hunkers down next to her, compacting his bulk into a boulder shape.

9

There is no way, Ruth thinks, and grits her teeth as she allows a few drops of urine to escape. She's wearing a pantyliner and it's one of the more absorbent ones, so hopefully that will help. As long as she only goes a little bit.

The lake glitters at them, hiding everything underneath. There are other docks, Ruth sees now, but they are spaced very far apart. Ensuring privacy. And there is a fast-moving dot in the distance, coming closer.

Fern yells, "Look!" She jumps up and races to the edge of the shore as the roar of an outboard motor obliterates all other sounds.

LESS THAN TEN minutes later, after Stef and Sammy docked their boat and piled out with the twins to greet Ruth and Fern, and Marvin told Stef to hurry up and let Ruth into the cottage already because she needed to use the facilities, and Sammy said he'd stay at the beach with the kids as long as Stef brought him down some beef jerky—"The spicy one! Not the regular one because it tastes like a dead rat." And all three girls collapsed together in a heap, helpless with laughter: "He said dead rat! He said dead rat!"—Ruth sits on the toilet, relieved at last, and looks down between her pale legs.

The bowl is bright with ribbons of blood. And here she'd thought she was nearly done. She should've packed tampons but she only brought the pads. That's all she thought she would need.

She glances around the room but there's no medicine cabinet, and the sink is a fancy pedestal one with no cupboard underneath. If she wants a tampon, she will have to ask. She hates asking Stef for anything.

She wipes one last time and stands up.

At their old apartment, the toilet used to clog regularly, and over the years she became an expert with the plunger. Wrestling with whatever came out of her, forcing it back down the pipes.

She holds her breath as she flushes, and she's grateful when everything disappears.

The distant shrieks just barely reach her. Fern is always so excited to see Amelia and Isabelle. They're her best friends, she says, even though the twins are seven and Fern isn't even four yet.

Ruth turns on the tap, and a loud knock at the bathroom door makes her flinch and fling a spray of cold water onto the round mirror, which has been designed to resemble a ship's porthole. The water streams down over her startled reflection and there's another knock, louder this time.

"Hello?" she calls.

"It's me," says Stef. "Just making sure you didn't fall in."

Ruth turns off the faucet and dries her hands, then swipes the fluffy hand towel across the glass, but of course that just makes everything worse. She could hunt around for cleaning products but she doesn't want to. Instead, she grabs a bottle of expensive-looking lotion and squeezes out a big glob. It's pale yellow and smells like lemons, and she's still rubbing it into her skin when she opens the door and smiles at her friend.

Stef smiles back and walks right in. "Do you love this place or what?"

She hustles Ruth back over to the sink and shoves until both of their faces are framed inside the decorative porthole.

Stef is also wearing a tank top, but hers fits much better than Ruth's does. It clings to her curves where Ruth's fabric sags or bunches up. It's a nicer colour too. The light blue complements

11

Stef's light hair, while Ruth's dark purple next to her dark brown hair just washes her out entirely.

She tries to stop comparing and focuses on the frame around them instead. It looks expensive, made of shiny brass and embellished with fake rivets and hinges.

"I like this thing." Stef taps the glass. "It reminds me of that work cruise we took that time."

Which one? thinks Ruth, and guesses, "When you and James got sick from the seafood salad at the buffet?" She remembers being a tiny bit glad when that happened, but then she felt guilty.

Stef nods grimly. "Goddamn clams in mayonnaise. What were we thinking?" Suddenly her eyes go wide with fear, and she claws at the mirror and yells, "Help us! We're sinking!" And chuckles at her own joke.

"Ha ha." Ruth takes a step backward. "I should get back to Fern."

"Oh, she's fine. Anyway, I have to give you the grand tour first." Stef scowls at the streaks on the mirror. "Ugh, look at this, Sammy is such a slob. He always flosses his teeth right up close and then tries to smear off his disgusting plaque morsels with toilet paper. I'll make him clean this later." She surveys the rest of the bathroom and gives Ruth a knowing smirk. "Bitch always has the worst timing, doesn't she?"

"What?" She follows Stef's gaze to the trash bin, where she thought she'd buried all the evidence. But there is the lilac wrapper with its crumpled, white wing, resting on the very top of the pile. "Oh, right."

She should've just bundled up everything in a wad of toilet paper and stuck it in her purse, because now Stef is going to say something like, *You better not go swimming with that thing stuck to your crotch or the muskies will start circling!* She can almost hear the words in the air already. The two of them have known each other for so long.

But all her friend says is, "You want a beer?"

STEF WALKS RUTH through every room in the cottage.

There's a finished basement with two guest bedrooms, where Ruth and Fern will be sleeping. There's also a bathroom downstairs, and a playroom with a giant TV in the centre of it. On the main floor is the kitchen, the adjoining living room with another big-screen TV, another bathroom down a short hall, and a big, screened porch and wraparound deck facing the water. On the top floor are two more bedrooms—one for Stef and Sammy and the other for the twins.

Ruth tries not to gape too much at how nice everything is, and nods politely but impatiently as her friend proudly points out the various features of each room and explains how the previous owners had been happy to give them most of the furniture and even left behind a bunch of toys for the twins— "They just wanted to get out of here, I guess. Lucky us!"

Finally the two mothers go back outside and start down the long staircase together, clutching their cold beer bottles.

Ruth grips the splintery railing with her free hand and follows her friend down to the beach, trying to make her feet move faster than they want to go.

"Whoa," Stef says over her shoulder, "what's the rush? You're on Cottage Time now."

"I just want to get back to Fern, that's all."

"Sammy's down there, don't worry about it. Sorry we were late, by the way. We lost track of time. But hey, you got to meet Marvin! Isn't he great?"

13

Ruth nods. "He offered to watch Fern while I peed in the bushes."

"See? What a guy."

"Except I don't know him, so I didn't think that was a good idea."

"I assume he told you *I* know him, though." Stef's voice tightens. "Right?"

"He did."

"Jesus, what's he going to do? You could've left her with him for a *minute*." Stef stops walking and turns around, so Ruth has to stop walking too. "Marvin's a weirdo, but he's harmless. He and his wife look after the twins sometimes. Do you think I'd let them babysit if I didn't trust him?"

"No," Ruth says quickly, "of course not." She hates the smallness of her voice.

The two of them stand there, surrounded by trees. Ruth thinks, stupidly, *This really is a beautiful spot.*

When she was a kid, her mom and dad rented a tiny cottage for two weeks every summer. It was just the three of them, and they'd let her stay up past her bedtime and eat Froot Loops and Jiffy Pop, and then her dad would take her out onto the dock to look at the stars. They used a flashlight to get there, but once they were sitting down, he switched it off. Then the night was all around them and the lake was going *swish-swish* and he'd point out the constellations to her, one by one.

"Exactly," says Stef. "They're good neighbours, which counts for a lot around here. Apparently we have to rely on our neighbours in cottage country—we've joined a *community*." She performs a dramatic shiver of revulsion, then turns and keeps going.

The laughter falls out of Ruth, like it always does. *Laughing is good*, she thinks. *It makes everything easier.*

From somewhere down below, a few elated squeals drift up. More happy sounds.

"His wife, Lesley, is big into baking pies," Stef goes on. "She's got time for shit like that because they don't have kids. She made us a peach one after we moved in and Marvin carried it over on his paddleboard."

Ruth tries to see what the girls are doing, but the foliage is thick on both sides so there's only green. "How was it?"

"I have no idea. It sat on the counter for a few days and then I threw it out." Stef points at something grey as they round a bend. "Watch yourself there."

When she sees what Stef is talking about, Ruth skids on some loose gravel and sucks in a breath. "Oh."

The wasps' nest is hanging from a low branch, ugly and bulging and too close to the stairs.

"Fern's never been stung before," she says.

"Yeah, neither have the twins." Stef waves a dismissive hand as they pass by. "It's fine. Just steer clear of them and they'll steer clear of you."

"Okay." Ruth frowns as she focuses on her descent. "If you say so." She's almost sure she can hear buzzing behind them.

The girls' squeals intensify as they get closer to the beach.

"Mommmmyyyyy!"

"I'm here, Fern!" she calls, quickening her pace.

She's nearly at the bottom now. Only a few more steps to go.

And then at last she has an unobstructed view, and there is her child. Hurtling across the beach with Amelia and Isabelle. Because Marvin is chasing them.

Ruth's voice is sharp: "Stef, where's Sammy?"

"How am I supposed to know?"

In her rush to reach her daughter, Ruth trips on the final stair and lands with a grunt. Her beer bottle goes flying and shatters on a rock.

Now the sand around her is full of broken glass.

"Mommy!" hollers Fern. "We're playing monster!"

Only a few metres away, the three girls swerve toward them.

"Stay there!" Ruth shouts. "Don't move!"

Stef stops behind her. "I knew I should've given you a can. I was just going to slum it with a couple Bud Light Limes, but no, you made me get the fancy microbrews from the back of the fridge."

"Is there a snake, Mommy?" Fern is standing perfectly still between Amelia and Isabelle.

Closer to the water, Marvin is bent over, fiddling with his feet. "No snakes," he says. "Just a teeny accident." He straightens up and strides over in flippers, wielding a pink plastic rake and a yellow plastic bucket, both instruments tiny in his giant hands.

The little girls giggle uproariously as he shuffles past them.

"You're awesome," Stef tells him, with a sideways glance at Ruth.

He shrugs away the compliment and begins sifting through the sand with the rake, picking up the jagged amber shards and dropping them into the bucket, which is adorned with a cartoon frog in a coconut bra and hula skirt.

Ruth stays absolutely still as he crouches next to her and lays his palms on the sand and sweeps cautious circles all around her until he's satisfied the danger is gone.

When she and her dad were done looking at the stars, they always made their way back to the cottage without the flashlight. "Because our eyes have adjusted," he would say. "We can see in the dark now, just like the nocturnal animals." She held his hand, which was so much larger than hers and always warm. She walked along the path carefully, startled the whole way by all the outside noises she wasn't used to. "It's okay," he'd say. "You're safe." And she was.

"All clear." Marvin offers a hand to help her up. "And the other good news is, Sammy's in the boathouse right now restocking the beer fridge."

"Oh, shit," says Stef. "I forgot his beef jerky."

Ruth lets Marvin pull her to her feet. "Looks like you saved the day," she tells him.

"Does that mean I can stay here with you guys?" His voice is pleading, over the top. "I don't want to go home yet."

"What do you say, Ruth?" says Stef. "Should we let him stay?"

"Mommy?" calls Fern. "Is it safe now?"

Ruth nods, and her daughter rockets over and snuggles against her legs. She reaches down and rubs Fern's back. "Sure, why not."

The grin Marvin gives her is so wide, it nearly splits his handsome face in two. "I knew you liked me."

She sees the streak of red then, bright against her child's skin, and gasps.

"Don't worry, it's from me. From when I helped you up." Marvin displays his bleeding hand, and winces as he picks out the tiniest piece of glass.

RUTH SMOOTHS THE beach towel over the sand for her and Fern. Fern doesn't like it when there are lumps underneath. If James were here with them, he'd be giving Ruth the look that said, *Don't worry about it.*

She gives up and sits down and pulls Fern onto her lap so the lumps won't offend her immediately.

Marvin is smiling at her over the lid of Stef and Sammy's cooler, just a few feet away. "Here you go," he says, and extends his arm to hand her a shiny can of beer. "A prize for the best mom in town."

"Oh. Thanks." She takes it from him and their fingertips touch for the briefest instant, and heat crawls up her neck and cheeks and makes her hairline prickle with moisture.

"Where's your bathing suit?" he asks her. "Don't you like to swim?"

"Not today." She should've changed into shorts when she was inside. It's way too hot for jeans. She presses the cold aluminum against her forehead and gazes at the sparkling lake.

He's still looking at her. "You're an interesting specimen."

Fern cuddles closer, wrapping her arms around Ruth's middle. "She's my mommy!"

"That's me." Ruth bends forward, hiding behind her curtain of dark hair, and brushes her lips against the top of Fern's fluffy, yellow head. Feather-soft at first but then with more pressure, to remind herself that her daughter is right here, in kissing distance.

Marvin gets up and walks over to sit down beside them. "Lucky girl," he says, and she isn't sure which one of them he's talking about.

Nearby, Stef and Sammy lay out their own brightly coloured beach towels. Then Sammy starts blowing up an inflatable raft while the twins fling sand toys into the air and screech in protest over Stef's sunscreen-application attempts. She snaps at their bathing-suit straps and slaps on some lotion, but they wriggle free before she can rub it in.

Then Stef looks over at Ruth and Marvin and Fern, and for a moment she stands completely still with her hands on her hips, watching them, before she plunges back into the fray.

A few days earlier, Stef had called Ruth from the cottage and said, "My family is driving me crazy. I love them but I want to kill them. We just had Sammy's brother and his wife here, and they provided zero relief because all they wanted to do was talk about what life will be like when the baby comes, and I said, 'Here's your preview. It will be hell. Now shut up and talk about something else.' But they never did. And of course Beth-Anne wasn't boozing but Danny wouldn't touch a drop either because he's doing this solidarity thing, which is super annoying if you ask me, but whatever. So you have to come up. I need to drink more, and if you guys are here then I'll have an excuse to go through more wine without feeling like I have a problem. And you should stay for a week because the summer's almost over and I really want to show the place off and brag about how we own this gigantic piece of useless land in the godforsaken wilderness now."

"Ha ha," Ruth said into the phone. She was surrounded by unpacked boxes in the kitchen of their new house, assembling the ingredients for high-fibre, low-sugar energy balls. She'd found the recipe in a parenting magazine, which proclaimed they were full of nutrition and a "no-fail hit" with kids. The accompanying photo, of a plate piled high with glistening brown nuggets, had turned her stomach.

"Seriously," said Stef, "you have to see this place. It looks like an actual Swiss chalet. But without the tasty chicken and fries and that sauce they have that's straight out of heaven and the fingerbowls for rinsing your greasy chicken-hands afterwards. So basically a chalet with none of the good things about a chalet."

19

Stef and Sammy had bought the cottage at the start of the summer, shortly after Ruth and James had signed the mortgage for their new house. Nearly every day since, Stef had bugged Ruth and James to drive up for a visit, and Ruth kept coming up with reasons not to go.

"It sounds great," she said, "but we're still settling in here, and I'm pretty busy getting Fern ready for kindergarten . . ."

From the family room down the hall, Fern started giggling at whatever was happening on *Puppy Commander*, and Ruth checked the clock and realized she'd lost track of how long the TV had been on. She tried to ignore the stab of guilt as she counted out twenty cashews. *Or was it thirty?* If it was thirty, she didn't have enough. She checked the recipe again. *Goddammit.*

"Are you kidding me?" Stef snorted. "Take the child to Old Navy and let her pick out a new outfit for the first day. Boom. She's ready. Now get packing."

"I don't mean buying stuff—" She stopped, because Stef would laugh at her. She meant reading books about starting kindergarten, exploring the schoolyard together, showing Fern the door she would take to her classroom. Reassuring her and preparing her. Ruth jammed her phone between her shoulder and her ear so she could dump two cups of rolled oats into the mixing bowl. "We've just been talking about what it will be like," she said. "So she won't be scared."

"Why would she be scared? The twins will be there."

Because they all lived in the same neighbourhood now, like a big, happy family. Just two months ago, Stef had been walking to the park with the twins. "They were going stupid-slow," she told Ruth and James later, "and I was yelling at them to hurry the hell up and then we turned the corner and ta-da! There it was." She texted a photo of the for-sale sign to James, and later that same day he and Ruth were bidding on the place with the real estate agent Stef had found for them, and then they were moving out of their cozy apartment on the other side of town and moving into a big, echoey house right around the corner from their closest friends.

James had strolled into the kitchen then and plucked the phone away from Ruth. "Hello, Stef? Did you just invite us to your cottage again?" A pause. "Thank you very much. We're looking forward to it."

Ruth snatched her phone back from him as Stef was saying, "Thank *God*. Forests are boring and I'm completely miserable without you."

Without who? Ruth had wanted to say, but Stef had already hung up.

She set her phone down on the counter and scowled at James. "Why did you do that?"

"Because I love you but you're stressing me out, so I'm forcing you to take a vacation." He leaned over to sniff at the brown sludge in their food processor. "What's this?"

Ruth scowled harder. "Date syrup."

"Why?"

"Because I want our daughter to be healthy."

"Ah."

She crossed her arms. "It's going to be delicious."

"I'm not disagreeing with you."

"Really?"

"Ruthie. Come on." James grabbed her elbow and pulled her into a hug.

"She wants us to stay for a whole week. That's a long time. And we'll get back right before school starts. I wanted more time to get ready."

"You have all those happy memories of going to a cottage with your folks when you were little, right? Now Fern will too." He grinned. "And aren't you always saying she needs more fresh air, and that being out in nature is good for her *health*?"

"Yes, but—"

A fresh round of frenzied cartoon barking issued from the family room, followed by Fern's hysterical laughter, and Ruth sighed.

"How about you and Fern go ahead and I'll stay behind and finish the unpacking?" he said. "Then everything will be done when we come back home."

For a moment she was frozen, limbs thick with indignation. Then she relented and rested her head against his chest. "I still have to buy Fern a lunch bag."

"I'll buy the lunch bag."

"It has to be cute. And insulated. And we need mini ice packs. And we'll miss you."

"Check, check, check. And I'll be there after a day or two." He kissed her. "We're going to have fun."

Now it's the late afternoon on a lovely day and the sun is beating down and James isn't here and Ruth would rather be anywhere else, but she shouldn't think that because they're with their friends on a free holiday and Fern is sitting in her lap, waving a pink shovel at her and asking, "Will you dig with me, Mama?"

"Of course." She smiles and takes the shovel, bumping her thumb across the tiny rubber hearts on its handle. "I would love to dig with you."

Stef glowers as the twins dodge her lotion-covered hands again. "Fine, you two want to burn? Then burn. Go play."

The two girls stick out their pointy tongues and galumph off.

Ruth has already slathered her own daughter in chalky, all-natural sunblock. Now Fern's warm, sticky, organic-coconut-smelling body is making her sweat even more as she shoves the toy spade into the sand.

Stef wipes her palms on her thighs, leaving matching white streaks, and grabs a beer from the cooler. The can hisses when she pops it open. "Here's to Cottage Time."

"To Cottage Time!" Sammy and Marvin shout in unison.

Ruth yawns, and Stef arches an eyebrow. "Are we keeping you up?"

"It was a long drive," says Ruth. "And I'm old."

"You're not old. You're the same age as me." Stef turns to their neighbour. "How old are you, Marvin?"

"Old enough to know better." He winks at her. "Or forty-six, if you want to get specific."

"Ahhh!" She reels back, cackling gleefully. "You're like our dad!"

Sammy rolls his eyes. "He's four years older than us."

"To the forties!" Stef raises her can again. "The golden age of wisdom, rugged good looks, and not giving a fuck."

Ruth coughs, widening her eyes in Fern's direction.

"She's oblivious," says Stef. "Don't worry about it."

Ruth takes a long sip of her beer and abandons the shovel. Fern hands her a green plastic turtle mould next, and she fills it with sand and tamps it down as Amelia and Isabelle wade into the lake together, holding hands.

At the beginning of the summer, the two families had cele-brated the new cottage and the new house with a barbecue in Stef and Sammy's backyard, which was now only a few back-yards away from Ruth and James's. The adults were drinking margaritas on the patio and the children were playing "dog,"

23

which meant they were taking turns tying a skipping rope around each other's waists and yanking on it.

Ruth had said, as she often did, "It must be nice, having twins."

"Oh yeah," Stef had sputtered. "It's awesome!"

"Every time we cross the road or go to the playground or do anything, we basically wait for one of them to die," said Sammy. "Because it's impossible to watch them both at the same time. They're so fast."

"And stupid," said Stef.

Sammy nodded. "Yeah, really dumb."

"It's not like I planned it this way, obviously." Stef shook her head as their three girls ran around the yard, barking. "I only wanted one, but my uterus got greedy."

James had laughed and laughed.

But Ruth had swallowed a mouthful of sour ice and said, "But they keep each other company. With an o-n-l-y c-h-i-l-d, you worry about them being lonely all the time."

"She can't hear us," James told her. "You don't have to spell."

"The grass is always greener," said Stef. "But when you're the only kid, your friends are your family. You and James and I all figured that out, right?"

Ruth shrugged. "I guess we did."

"And so will Fern. And if she doesn't, there's always booze. For you, I mean. Not for her. That would be bad parenting." Stef raised her glass, grinning. "And now you're within stumbling distance from us, so you can drink even more!"

Fern had looked over at them then, and she had the rope around her neck. As Ruth bolted toward her, she asked, "What grass is greener, Mama? I want to see it. And I'm not lonely right *now*."

Sammy's cheeks balloon out with his last few breaths into the air mattress. He's sitting cross-legged on the sand with it, bending forward at an awkward angle. His eyes are bulging and his face is red with the exertion.

"Ooh," says Stef, "slide that over here when you're done, big boy."

He jams in the plug and shakes a victorious fist in the air, then flops down onto the raft with a mournful sigh and rubs his hairy belly. "My sweet, salty, dehydrated beef, how I yearn for you."

"Fine, be that way." Stef glares at him, then says to Marvin and Ruth, "Did you hear about that comedian who died? That adorable short guy from that show? His torso was almost non-existent but I was totally in love with him."

"He hanged himself," says Sammy. "Stopped being funny real fast after that."

"That's too bad." Marvin takes a long sip of his beer. "He must've had a good reason, though."

"Whoa, welcome to Downer Town," says Stef. "I'm trying to talk about comedy here. Also throbbing carnal desire."

"He's dead." Sammy tosses a handful of sand at her. "I'm all you've got left."

Stef unleashes a melodramatic wail. "But I *miss* him!"

Sammy rolls his eyes and gets another beer.

A few seagulls are circling overhead, screeching at them.

Marvin glances up at the birds and then gets to his feet. He moves a few paces away from the other adults and Fern, closer to the twins and their laughter and splashing.

Isabelle and Amelia keep playing, running back and forth through the shallow water. They notice Marvin and whisper something to each other. All at once they sprint out of the lake and over to his paddleboard that he's left on the sand. They hold hands and start jumping up and down on it, looking directly at him the whole time.

He doesn't react to their antics. He doesn't smile. He just stands there as the gulls wheel and scream above them.

Stef and Sammy are still focused on taunting each other and they haven't seen any of it.

Fern stares up at Ruth, pulling her attention back. "Who's dead, Mama?"

Instead of answering, Ruth lifts the plastic mould to reveal a perfectly formed sand turtle. "Look what Mommy made!"

"Ooh," Fern coos. "I think it's a baby."

Stef whacks Sammy's arm. "You're just jealous because you can't tell a joke to save your life."

Marvin turns around and walks back to the group, and he's smiling again. "These guys crack me up," he tells Ruth. "They're a riot, the way they pretend to fight. I love it."

"Nothing pretend about it, my friend." Sammy blows Stef a kiss and she mimes choking on it, bugging out her eyes and clawing at her throat.

"See what I mean?" Marvin slaps his thigh. "When my wife and I argue, we do it for real. That's why I like coming over here. Life's too short." He sits down and says, almost as an after-thought, "I do love her, though."

"All couples fight," says Stef, her eyes on Ruth. "Even the perfect ones."

Ruth stares at the beads of condensation on her icy can. As soon as she wipes one away, another one takes its place. This annoys her more than it should, and she keeps on wiping.

"So," says Marvin, "how do you all know each other?"

"Ruth and I went to school together," Stef tells him.

"Ah, so you two go way back. I bet you wild girls got up to a few naughty things in your time, right?"

"Primary school!" Stef yells. "We met in kindergarten, you creepy man."

"Oops," says Marvin. "But I bet you've gotten up to some trouble since then, though, eh?"

"Smooth," says Stef. "And yes."

Fern whispers, "What naughty things did Auntie Stef do?"

Ruth pictures Stef and James alone in a room somewhere. In multiple rooms. In dormitories and offices, on boats and islands. They spend so much time together, and they know each other so well.

She shakes her head at herself and whispers back, "They're just being silly."

"We were the only onlies in our class," Stef tells Marvin. "And all the kids with siblings were weird."

"I thought some of them were nice," says Ruth.

"Yeah," says Stef, "but I was the best."

"*Anyway*," says Sammy, "if it was really an actual life-or-death situation, I could tell a joke. I know lots of jokes. I'm a joke machine."

"Knock, knock!" Fern shouts.

Marvin leans toward her. "Who's there?"

Ruth thinks, *Too close.*

"Barry."

"Barry who?"

"Barry the treasure where no one can find it!"

And Marvin roars. He doubles over with mirth, too much, too loud.

But Fern laughs too, which means everything must be okay.

"*Barry*, like *bury*," says Marvin. "That's brilliant."

Sammy's phone jingles. He squints at the screen and then holds it up. "Bev and Wally calling!"

Stef groans. "Isabelle! Amelia! Geema and Geepa want FaceTime!"

"Yay!" The twins run over and snatch the phone from their dad's hand and immediately start chattering to it.

"We could go to the moon and they'd track us down." Stef shakes her head, but she's smiling. "There's no escape."

"That reminds me," says Ruth. "Mom says hi."

"Aww, isn't that sweet. Tell her hi back. No, wait. Tell her *hello*." Stef exaggerates the last word, drawing it out. Making it oddly formal. "Tell her I miss her and I hope she's holding up and all that."

"Okay, I will. Thanks." Ruth nods. "How are your folks doing?" The question skips out of her, too lightly.

"How do you think?" Stef asks sharply, and Ruth winces.

She looks down, fiddling with a knot in Fern's hair. "I wouldn't know."

Stef stares at the lake. "Yeah, well, neither would I."

"Stop it, Mommy!" Fern jerks her head away from Ruth's hands.

"Sorry, honey," she murmurs.

"Hey," says Sammy, "did you guys see that YouTube video with the wiener dog that runs into the ocean with the GoPro strapped to its neck?"

"It wasn't an ocean," Stef says. "It was a lake."

"And that's important to the story *how*?" Sammy gives her a look, then shouts, "Girls! Give me my phone back!"

Amelia gallops over and tosses it to him. "Geema and Geepa were being boring so we hung up on them," she says, and runs back to her sister.

Ruth finishes her beer and sets the empty can down in the sand. The lake shimmers, beckons.

Her daughter squirms in her lap, trying to find the most comfortable spot, and Ruth makes an irritated face before she can stop herself.

"Hey, hey!" James had said a few weeks ago, when the three of them were at a public pool and Ruth had made the same face without even realizing it. He'd seized Fern out of her arms and tickled her until she squealed. "Why don't you swim with Daddy for a bit? Let's give Mommy a break."

Fern had furrowed her brow. "Why does Mommy need a break?"

"Well," he said, "there are a million reasons. Which one would you like to hear first?"

Ruth's jaw tightened. *I was fine*, she'd wanted to say. *We were fine*. But instead she just flipped onto her back, kicking her feet and windmilling her arms until she was in the deep end, all the way at the other side of the pool.

They'd gone swimming to escape the new house, which was crowded with boxes and all the work they had to do to make it feel like a home, and Ruth didn't want to do any of it. She'd neatly organized and clearly labelled all of Fern's things when she'd packed them, but she'd been haphazard with her own stuff and now she couldn't find anything when she needed it. She missed their little apartment on the other side of town and she wanted James to miss it too. But he kept going on about how great the new place was and how lucky they were that Stef had found it for them, and then Ruth had made that face and he had no idea why.

She stayed in the deep end for a while, treading water while James and Fern splashed each other and laughed and

29

waved at her. And eventually she swam back over because she missed them.

"What happens to the dog?" Marvin asks Sammy.

"Nothing. It just runs into the water." He aims a pointed look at his wife. "It doesn't matter what kind of water it is."

"Uh-huh," says Stef.

Over by the dock, Isabelle is examining an object on the sand. Then Amelia walks over with a stick and starts poking at whatever's there.

Stef leans sideways to drape an arm over her husband's shoulders, and plants a wet kiss on his gleaming bald head. "Look at our gorgeous, golden offspring with their terrifying praying-mantis bodies."

He barks out a laugh, shrugging her off. "Their knees and elbows are extremely pointy, it's true."

"Stop that," says Marvin. "They're just right."

"Okay, okay." Stef holds up her hands. "*Her* child is too cute to live, though." She nods over at Ruth and Fern. "She's like an elf crossed with a duckling."

"I'd say that's a fair assessment." Marvin gives Fern another wink, and she scowls at him and Stef.

"I'm not a duck," she says, and finally climbs off Ruth and moves away to sit by herself.

As soon as she's gone, Ruth aches for her, even though she's more comfortable now.

Marvin says, "So does the dog go swimming, or what?"

"It's not one of those ones where the animal gets h-u-r-t, is it?" says Ruth.

Stef pats her hand. "You don't have to spell. She's not paying attention."

Fern is digging a shallow trench in the sand, tongue stuck out in deep concentration.

"Wiener dogs have those stubby legs, right," says Sammy, "so it goes under really fast. But I don't think the dog drowns or anything. At least, they don't show that part."

Next, Fern carefully lines up rocks along the edge of her ditch.

"Here, I'll find it for you." Sammy starts tapping at his phone.

Nearly instantaneously, Amelia and Isabelle are racing over, shouting, "Video! Video!" Amelia is still carrying the stick, but now there's something on the end of it.

"And now you have to jump," says Fern. "I'm sorry, but you have to." Then she places a finger on each of the rocks in turn, and pushes.

31

"Okay, here you go." Sammy passes his phone to Marvin.

"You girls want to watch it with me?" Marvin asks, and it takes Ruth a moment before she realizes he's talking to the kids.

"Fern doesn't need to see it," she says. "Thanks."

"Then she can play with *this*!" trills Isabelle, and she grabs the stick from her sister's hand, and Ruth can see now that the thing on the end of it is a dead fish. Most of the body has rotted away, but the backbone and tail are still stubbornly attached to the head.

Now it's a puppet with pursed lips and empty eyeholes bobbing toward her terrified daughter, who crab walks backward to get away from it.

Ruth waits for Stef or Sammy to step in, but her friends just drink their beer as the twins slink closer and closer to Fern, ponytails swishing.

"Kiss me, kiss me, kiss me!" Amelia rasps, hiding her face behind the fish's.

"That's enough," Ruth says, loudly, but nobody pays attention.

Then Marvin shouts, "Hey, it's on now, you're going to miss it!" waving the shiny silver device like a flare.

And all at once, the sisters lose interest in their game and hurry over to him, dropping the stick and resting their chins on each of his shoulders. Folding their skinny arms and legs around him in an effort to get the best possible view.

Ruth picks up Fern and hugs her so tightly that she squawks, "Put me down, Mama!" But she doesn't. Not yet.

After all the anticipation, the clip is exactly what Sammy said it would be. Someone straps a camera to a dachshund's neck, and then the perspective switches to the dog's as it runs into some water and is quickly submerged.

When it's over, Marvin hands the phone back to Sammy and nods. "Yep, that's a good one."

THEY STAY ON the beach until dinnertime, and then everyone heads back up to the cottage.

It's silly to call it a cottage, really, because the place is huge.

It feels small right now, though, with all of them crowding in from outside. Stef and Sammy go to the kitchen and Amelia and Isabelle prowl around the living room in their wet bathing suits and drip all over the glossy wood floor. Ruth and Fern huddle together in the middle of everything and Marvin towers over them, taking up space with his wide shoulders and wider grin.

"Go upstairs and get some dry clothes on," Stef tells the twins.

"Not yet!" shouts Amelia.

"We want chips!" shouts Isabelle.

"I'm making a salad." Stef uncaps a bottle of Havana Club. "Are your legs broken?"

"No," says Isabelle, "somebody chopped them off and there's blood everywhere."

"Jesus Christ." Stef rolls her eyes and starts pouring drinks.

Sammy opens the fridge and pulls out a plate stacked with glistening slabs of raw meat. "Hello, my rib-eye children. I am going to cook you and eat you now."

Fern is gaping at Isabelle. "I don't see any blood."

Ruth strokes Fern's cheek. "She was just joking."

"Sammy?" says Stef. "A little help?"

"Don't look at me." Sammy grabs a barbecue lighter from the counter and squeezes the trigger, then makes a show of blowing out the flame. "The grillmeister must grill." He points the lighter at Marvin. "And the grillmeister's assistant must assist."

"If I must," says Marvin, "I must."

On his way to the screen door, Sammy slips on a small puddle of lake water. His arms shoot out and he finds his balance, but drops the steak plate. It breaks on the floor and splatters the wall with red.

Isabelle smirks. "I told you there was blood everywhere."

"Isabelle! Amelia!" Stef shouts. "Take. Those. Wet. Suits. Off. Right. Now!"

Amelia sneers at her. "Fine." She flicks a look at her sister, and in one coordinated motion, the twins strip off their suits in the middle of the living room. Then they seize each other's hands and whirl around and around, shrieking.

Fern stares at them, and so does Ruth.

The girls' bodies are luminous blurs of sharp angles and soft curves, with shoulder-blade wings and the faint outlines of ribs like long, clutching fingers. Their white teeth flash and their long hair flies, and Ruth wants to whirl with them.

They keep dancing in their tight circle, reckless and free and absolutely connected, and Ruth grasps her own daughter's hand and pulls her toward the living room. But stops.

Because Marvin is staring too. His mouth even hangs open slightly.

Then Stef breaks the spell and yells, "Upstairs, you two!"

The twins finally obey and scurry off.

Sammy gets a new plate and crouches over the fallen meat. Each piece makes a gentle sucking sound when he picks it up.

"Grillmeister, let's go," he tells Marvin, who nods, and the two men head out to the deck.

"Well, fuck." Stef walks over with a tumbler of rum and Coke and a dustpan. "That was exciting."

Fern yawns, and Ruth picks her up and holds her close. "Let's get out of here," she says, and they go.

RUTH DRAPES FERN'S dry towel over the couch in the play-room downstairs and then helps Fern out of her swimsuit in the bathroom, and her naked child stands before her with her little arms crossed. "You said we would go swimming but we didn't."

"I know, honey. I'm sorry. We'll swim tomorrow, okay?"

Fern sighs. "Okay." Her small shoulders slump like James's do when he's disappointed.

She also has her father's pale-blue eyes, and she's blonde like him too. Whenever Ruth searches her daughter for evidence of herself, she always comes up empty. "She has your eyelashes," James likes to joke. Even though she doesn't, not really.

"It's getting late," she tells Fern. "Maybe we should put your pyjamas on?"

Fern nods, and her compliance makes Ruth hopeful. But then she starts to pull the pyjama shirt over Fern's head and

Fern yanks it back up. "No!" The fabric stretches around her seething face, the neck opening wide and pulling the soft skin tight. "I can do it myself!"

"Okay, okay." Ruth holds up her hands, taking a few steps back.

"And I want privacy."

"Oh." She stops. "Are you sure?"

The clouds in her daughter's eyes darken, the wind whipping up. "Get out!"

"I'm going." Ruth lays the pyjama pants by the tiny, wiggling toes. "I'll be right outside, okay?" She pulls the door shut gently and hopes Fern doesn't notice when she wedges her foot in at the bottom to stop her from using the lock.

Then she stands in the empty playroom and waits.

Above them, the twins' feet pound across the floor. Back and forth, wildly, like they're chasing each other.

After several minutes, Fern pulls open the door and runs out of the bathroom, triumphant and resplendent in her pink-and-purple baby-hedgehog-parade sleep set, and yells, "Look at me!"

And Ruth applauds and tells her daughter what a good job she did and hugs her, and her daughter hugs her back.

Then Fern pulls away, and a shadow flits across her proud face as the cute cartoon creatures march all over her soft arms and legs and belly, their sharp spines poking holes through their own pyjamas. "Is it bedtime now?"

"Not yet." Ruth smiles. "We have to feed you first."

The twins barrel down the stairs then and start squabbling over who gets to play with the mom doll in the gargantuan dollhouse that sits in the darkest corner of the playroom.

"You broke off her arm last time!" shouts Isabelle.

35

"It was an accident!" Amelia screams back.

Fern skips over to them. "Can I play too?"

"Playing is stupid." Isabelle gives the dollhouse a kick and flops onto the couch. "Hey," she says, "why is this here?" She reaches behind her and yanks on Fern's towel.

"Leave it alone." Fern's voice deepens, full of authority that Ruth has never heard before. "That's mine."

"Whatever." Isabelle throws it back where it was. "Let's watch TV."

"Mama?" Fern asks, back to her regular high-pitched squeak, "can I watch a show?"

"Hmm, I don't know." Ruth glances at Amelia, who's rummaging through a toy doctor kit. She finds a plastic scalpel and grabs a nearby teddy bear and saws and slashes with grim determination, then tosses the bear aside in disgust when the dull blade fails her. "We should probably go up for dinner."

Isabelle is flipping through channels and doesn't look away from the television when she speaks. "We're having KD down here."

"What's that, Mommy?" says Fern.

"Please don't tell me that the child has never eaten Kraft Dinner before." Stef comes down the stairs with a giant bowl of chips and presents it to Fern, who sits on the floor and cradles the bowl in her lap, wide-eyed.

"I don't know," Ruth hears herself saying. "Maybe once or twice?"

"Nope," Fern pronounces. "Never."

Stef snorts. "Hilarious, but sadly unsurprising."

"Fern," Ruth prompts, "what do you say?"

She blinks up at her mother and then down at the chips. "Thank you."

"Such lovely manners." Stef points at the twins. "Ask Fern what she wants to watch. Fern is our guest."

"But we want to watch *The Bog Princess*!" says Isabelle.

Fern says, "I like *Puppy Commander*."

"*Puppy Commander* is for babies," says Amelia.

"I'm not a baby." Fern eats some chips. "I'm a big girl."

Stef looks at Ruth.

Ruth shrugs. "As long as it's not s-c-a-r-y."

"I've never actually seen it," Stef says. "But it's a movie about a mermaid. How scary can a mermaid be?"

Amelia and Isabelle start jumping up and down on the couch. "Bog Princess! Bog Princess!"

"Okay, just shut up about it!" Stef finds the movie and starts it. "Goddamn Netflix."

Ruth hunches down next to Fern. "Do you want me to stay down here with you?"

Fern scowls and struggles to her feet with the massive chip bowl. "I'm a big girl," she says again, and strides over to the couch to sit awkwardly between the bouncing twins.

"You heard her." Stef grins at Ruth and starts up the stairs.

Isabelle and Amelia drop down on either side of Fern and shove their hands into the chip bowl, and then all three of them sit staring together at the flickering screen with big eyes and chomping mouths.

Ruth follows Stef slowly. At the top of the stairs, she ducks her head down for one more look and then leaves the basement door open.

Stef goes to the kitchen and takes a bag of lettuce out of the fridge.

Ruth trails after her and stands stiffly, crossing and uncrossing her arms. "Fern's never really watched anything but *Puppy*

Commander. There's this puppy and it's in charge of its owner, or something. I think it's supposed to be funny but I don't really get it."

"Wait until she's seven." Stef rips open the bag and dumps the lettuce into a bowl. "You won't understand any of the shit she watches then."

"Do you want me to make the kids' food?"

Her friend snickers. "You can't even say it. Come on. Say 'mac and cheese.' I dare you."

"It's not a big deal." Ruth finds a pot and fills it with water. She shakes in some salt and thumps it onto the stove, then grabs a spoon to give it a completely unnecessary stir.

A burst of laughter from the screened porch makes her jump. Sammy and Marvin are out there, pouring wine and waving their knives around.

"KD boxes are in the cupboard next to the fridge." Stef frowns at the expiry date on a bottle of salad dressing and then douses the greens with it. "Now come and have a drink while the water's boiling."

"Okay," says Ruth.

She always says okay. Stef makes the plan and Ruth goes along with it. That's how they do things.

Stef carries the salad and the two of them file out to the screened porch, where Marvin and Sammy are drinking wine and eating steak. They're talking about a daycare they heard about in the news, where the workers forced the children to scratch and bite and kick each other and made the other kids sit in a circle and watch.

"That's not funny," says Ruth. "That's awful."

"That's what I said." Marvin pats the empty spot beside him at the picnic table, and Stef starts climbing over that bench.

"Hey," says Sammy, "I'm lonely over here!"

She rolls her eyes and retracts her long leg. "Fine."

Stef sits beside Sammy, and Ruth perches on the edge of the bench next to Marvin, who leans toward her and whispers, "That's what I was hoping would happen."

Ruth suddenly feels warm, even with the cool evening breeze blowing in.

She kept meaning to change into shorts but she's still wearing her jeans, which are squeezing her too tightly. Stef and Sammy have changed into T-shirts and loose, comfortable-looking linen pants. And Marvin is still shirtless.

He wouldn't have any clothes here, though, Ruth thinks. And Sammy is shorter and wider than he is so an offer to borrow a shirt probably wouldn't help. But now it's hard not to look at Marvin. He looks good.

Ruth drops a napkin onto her lap and fidgets with it, folding and unfolding the corners until creases form. "Your wife isn't coming for dinner?"

Marvin shakes his head. The palm trees on his shorts have smiley faces on them. "She doesn't like fun."

"Ha," she says, but she can't tell if he's joking or not.

"But seriously, that news story *was* kind of funny, right?" Sammy slides a plate in front of Ruth without asking how she likes her steak done. "Like a toddler fight club."

The meat is still bloody, which makes her feel ill, but she thanks him anyway.

"People are garbage," Marvin says, and pours her a big glass of red.

He's staring at her, so she looks out at the lake after she thanks him too.

Far down below, there's a steady shushing as waves slap

39

against the shore again and again, and tiny lights from distant cottages twinkle at them through the dark trees.

She takes a big swig. "That's why I didn't send Fern to day-care. Bad things can happen."

"I think it's safe to say that was an isolated incident." Stef spears a rib-eye off the serving platter and smacks it onto her plate. "James told me he wanted to at least find a part-time spot somewhere to give Ruth a break," she tells Marvin, "but she had to go and be all martyr-y about it for four years."

James told me.

Because he and Stef are such good buddies.

"I wanted to stay home with her," says Ruth. "I enjoy her company."

Marvin smiles at her. "That's sweet."

"Thanks." She focuses on her wine glass, her cheeks flushing.

"Fern's never even had a real babysitter," Stef goes on. "Can you believe it?"

"We don't know any teenagers," says Ruth. "And Fern has her grandparents. They look after her sometimes."

"Must be nice," Stef mutters.

"That's good," says Marvin. "Date nights are important."

"Oh, hell yes." Sammy nods at him. "If Bev and Wally weren't on the other side of the country, I would physically chain them to our children. This is why we're eternally grateful to you and Lesley." He pounds the table. "I need more unfettered sex with my wife!"

Marvin laughs. "What about your parents?" he asks Stef. "They don't live nearby?"

She drains her wine glass. "Oh, they live nearby. But they've got better things to do." She pokes Ruth in the arm. "Don't worry, we know plenty of teenagers. We'll hook you up."

James used to talk about how much Stef amazed him, after everything she'd been through with her parents. She could've been an asshole but she wasn't. She was always there for him, and Ruth too, and what was in it for her to be so nice? Nothing. But she was nice anyway. She was an only child like them, he'd always remind her, but their parents doted on them and Stef's mom and dad didn't give a shit that she existed. But she was still so positive, and so much fun.

And Ruth would ask in a flat voice if they could talk about something else for a change. Could they please stop talking about Stef and her amazing greatness, just for a few minutes?

He said to Ruth once, on their honeymoon, "You don't give her enough credit, you know."

They were drinking pina coladas under the thatched roof of a bar at their tropical resort, and the weather that day was perfect.

"For what?" The frozen cocktail was too sweet, and she pushed it away. "For rising above her terrible childhood? Give me a break. Her parents didn't abuse her, James. They were just busy." Even though that was bad enough, she knew. But Stef had survived. Ruth stared at the ocean over her new husband's slumped shoulder. "She got enough attention from my parents, anyway."

"Who's this James I keep hearing about?" Marvin asks.

Stef points her knife at Ruth. "Her hubby."

"Aha." He nods. "The mysterious missing husband in the big new house in Auntie Stef's neighbourhood, right?"

A fruit fly is swimming in Ruth's wine. The little legs are kicking uselessly. She dips a finger in and ferries the tiny body to one side, then crushes it against the glass. "That's him," she says, and wipes her finger on her napkin.

41

"They just moved!" Stef crows. "Ruth and I used to dream about growing up and getting houses on the same street. Didn't we, Ruthie?"

A slow nod. "We did."

"We were supposed to go to the same university too, but Ruth broke my heart and got accepted somewhere else. Silly girl. But then I met James and lured her back with him, and the rest is history. If it wasn't for me, she'd probably still be on the market."

Marvin glances sideways at Ruth. "Is that so?"

She shrugs and pulls the salad bowl toward her plate. Once she peers inside, though, she pushes it away. Stef used too much dressing and the vegetables are drowning in it.

For a few weeks after they started at their separate schools, Ruth and Stef had been farther apart than they'd ever been. Ruth missed her friend at first, but then she didn't. She made new friends and they stayed up all night talking passionately about ideas. It didn't even matter what the ideas were about because everyone's brains were exploding and the deepest conversations could be sparked by the simplest things. She didn't like beer yet so she drank vodka mixed with Crystal Light lemonade, which was awful but also really good. She flirted and laughed and ate too much junk food on dorm-room floors. She went to parties and concerts and played endless games of pinball in coffee shops. But then Stef wanted her to come and visit all the time, so she went.

And one of those times, a cute blond guy with pale-blue eyes wandered into Stef's dorm room and sat down next to Ruth on Stef's unmade single bed.

"Ruth, this is James," Stef told her. "He's a lonely only too."

"I'm not lonely." James smiled and stuck out his hand for Ruth to shake. "Actually, I take that back."

"We're just buddies," Stef had purred into her ear later that night. "But he wants me."

"A match made in heaven by a heavenly matchmaker." Stef grins around the table and stabs at the slick leaves of her salad. "James used to say to me, 'I really like this girl, but I'm not sure if I'm in the right headspace for a relationship.'" She mock-punches Ruth in the arm. "But I had your back, babe. I told him he'd better go out with you or else he'd be stuck with me!"

Ruth stiffens. She's heard this before but now Stef has a new audience.

Marvin isn't laughing, though. He's gazing out the window quietly.

Ruth carves up her big steak, slowly and methodically, until her plate is full of small pieces that she still doesn't feel like eating.

The words Stef doesn't say shimmer between them: *None of this would be possible without me.*

"And then of course you met *me*, and I swept you off your feet." Sammy leers at his wife. "Meaning I waited until you were passed out on my floor and then I tried to get you into my bed but you wouldn't move, so I just lay down next to you and whispered subliminal messages in your ear all night to stoke your desire for me."

"Yep." Stef rolls her eyes. "That's exactly how it went."

Marvin swirls the wine in his glass, being careful not to spill any. "Love is funny, isn't it?" he says. "The way it changes."

He sounds unhappy, and Ruth reaches out and touches her glass to his.

"To Cottage Time," she murmurs, but just to him, and his entire face lights up at the words.

After she and James started going out, Ruth used to interrogate him about his relationship with Stef. She never believed him when he said nothing had ever happened between them. Eventually he started getting angry when she asked, so she stopped. Even though she still wanted him to say the words. Because every other boy she'd ever known had always preferred her friend. That was how it had always been, so why would it be different now?

Ruth feels the wine working. She continues to sip her merlot or shiraz or whatever it is and her stomach warms and settles, waves of acid evaporating as the booze floods in. The calm spreads until it crowds out everything else, until there's nothing left inside her at all.

"Well?" says Stef. She's waiting for Ruth to say something.

"What?" She looks away from her friend to the red puddle on her plate. It would be rude to say she's not hungry, so she guzzles more wine instead.

"I said how happy are you? Now that we're all together?"

"Oh." They're all looking at her now. "Very happy."

Sammy shoves a hunk of meat in his mouth and says to Ruth, "When's the big guy coming up, anyway?"

"In a couple days," says Stef.

He raises an eyebrow at her. "Did I ask you?"

"Whatever. By the way, the main-floor bathroom mirror is gross so you better clean it off later."

"Why is that my fault?" says Sammy.

"Everything is your fault," says Stef.

Ruth's phone buzzes in her back pocket. She jumps and pulls it out, and grins at the text from James: *I miss you!*

She starts typing back and Stef hollers, "Rudeness!"

"I'll be right back. James is just checking in." She steps away from the table and heads for the kitchen. "I have to cook the pasta anyway."

"Oh Jaaaames!" Stef trills. "I loooove you!"

Ruth keeps walking and types, *I miss you too.*

She sets her phone on the counter and opens the cupboard next to the fridge, which contains rows of Kraft Dinner boxes. She selects one, opens it up and dumps it into the boiling water on the stove. The pot gurgles and steams, and then something that isn't macaroni floats to the surface.

Ruth stares dumbly at the white envelope, which she realizes must contain the cheese powder, and looks around for something to fish it out with. She doesn't want it to burst open when it's not supposed to.

There are no implements nearby that she can use, so she holds her breath and reaches in. The pain comes fast, but she perseveres and snags a corner of the packet and lifts it out. She pats it dry on a tea towel, then stands there sucking her red fingers like an idiot.

Her phone buzzes again and she grabs for it.

Stef says you guys are up to no good already.

She glances over at the screened porch, where Stef is typing away on her own phone, and frowns.

She turns the burner down so the pasta doesn't boil over before she replies, *Guess what? I'm making Kraft Dinner for Fern.*

Whoa. You ARE up to no good.

That makes her smile.

How is our little bug?

She fights the urge to run down and check on Fern immediately. Instead she types, *She's fine.*

When the horrible macaroni is ready, Ruth will serve it to the children and she will see that Fern is fine.

45

That's good.

She waits for James to ask how she is, but he doesn't, and then Marvin is walking toward her.

"Stef says you have no idea what you're doing so I'd better take over," he tells her.

Stef says Stef says Stef says.

Out on the porch, her friend lets out a loud, braying laugh.

"Oh," she says. "Thanks." Ruth stares at her tiny screen and then looks back at Marvin. "I'll just—"

"Go." He shoos her away. "Don't leave the mysterious husband hanging."

She carries her phone over to the basement doorway. The girls are watching their movie with the lights off so she can't see anything.

She types, *We're having fun.*

That's good. I'll be there soon.

That's good too.

She wonders if that made him smile, and she waits to see if he'll say anything else, but her screen stays empty.

She pockets her phone and edges down the stairs. The only sound is coming from the TV, which is loud. She thinks she hears a scream, but that can't be right. This is a kids' movie.

She reaches the bottom and tiptoes closer to the couch, coming up behind the girls, and sighs with relief when she sees the bright cartoon characters on the screen.

"Hi, Mama," whispers Fern.

"Hi, honey," Ruth whispers back. She stands still and watches the movie for a while. It seems innocent enough.

Then the stairs creak.

A hulking shadow looms above them and begins to creep down. Closer and closer.

The children shriek and huddle together, and Ruth's heart races as she hurries over to switch on the light.

"It's okay," she tells them. "It's only Marvin."

"Hi, kids!" He holds up three small bowls of bright orange pasta, which are dwarfed even more in his giant hands. "Who's hungry?"

All three children shout at once, "Me!"

Marvin chuckles as he gives them their bowls. The twins first, then Fern.

When she takes her bowl and his hands are free, he reaches for her.

Ruth's heart thumps harder and she takes a step toward them.

But he only taps Fern on the top of her head—once, twice. "Hey," he says, "I like your towel."

"Thank you." Fern beams at him. "It's my favourite."

Isabelle and Amelia look over then, away from their food and the television, taking in the exchange and staring at Fern's bright-yellow beach towel, which is emblazoned with lobsters wearing T-shirts. James gave it to Ruth a long time ago, after she first told him she was pregnant. He'd had that wonderful, crazed grin on his face when she unwrapped it, and when she looked confused, he said, "Let's shell-ebrate!"

It's a dumb towel, but Fern loves it anyway.

Marvin scuttles a spidery hand closer to her daughter, and all of Ruth's muscles tense. He taps one of the scarlet claws and jerks his hand back. "Ouch!" he yelps, and Fern falls sideways laughing.

Ruth thinks, *Lobsters only turn red after they've been boiled.*

"Shh!" the twins admonish them, and Fern settles back and fixes her eyes on the TV screen with its flashing colours—

purple and green and blue and a blast of pink—and eats her Kraft Dinner with a look of dazed rapture that Ruth has never seen before.

"They look like they're having fun," Marvin says when he and Ruth walk back over to the stairs. "Don't they?"

Instead of answering him, she says, "I just have to get something."

She leaves him there and goes to Fern's bedroom to switch on the baby monitor she'd brought from home. Then she goes to her own room and unplugs the receiver by her bed. She holds it tight and wraps the cord around her other hand.

Marvin smiles when she returns, and they climb the stairs together.

"I like how careful you are with her," he says when they get to the top.

"Thank you." She only realizes then that she didn't remind Fern to thank him for dinner. It's too late now, though.

They walk through the cottage to the screened porch and Marvin shortens his long stride to match hers.

His breath is suddenly shallow, and Ruth wants to ask him if he's all right but she doesn't because there is something about his expression that stops her from saying anything. A thin wire stretches tightly between them, connecting them for this moment, and she sinks into their shared silence until Stef's voice shatters it into a million pieces.

"What took you so long?" she shouts. "We were about to start eating each other!"

"That doesn't even make sense," says Ruth. "You already ate."

"Oh, good lord," says Stef. "I was being crude."

"The crudest," Sammy says, and gives his lips an exaggerated lick.

48

"I think we just lost our PG rating," Marvin quips to Ruth, and she laughs.

"Ahh, I see how it is. Marvin's jokes are funnier than mine now, right?" Stef reaches for the wine bottle. "Look at you two, getting all cozy."

Ruth decides to ignore her, but when she sits at the picnic table next to Marvin, the heat from his bare skin is blazing and the triangle of hair on his chest is close to her eye level and she tries to shift farther away but there's no room to go anywhere.

"You want to borrow a shirt, buddy?" Sammy asks, and Ruth squirms even more with the fact of Marvin's half-nakedness being acknowledged like this, even though she's not even looking at him at all.

She's looking at Stef, who's smirking, and Ruth grabs her own wine glass and finishes the few drops that are left inside.

"I wonder what James is doing right now," her friend muses. "He should be here having fun with us but instead he stayed home like a good little husband. We'll have to catch him up on all our adventures when he finally gets here."

Marvin has been quietly eating the rest of his steak while they've been talking, but now he puts down his knife and fork and says, "My wife and I were at a mall last summer and something happened."

"Whoa." Sammy grips the table. "I'm on the edge of my seat already."

Marvin gives him the barest hint of a smile. "It was back in the city where we used to live before we sold our house and moved up here for good. We were in the food court, eating some kind of crap."

Sammy gestures grandly at the bloody scraps left on their plates. "So, not gourmet fare like this, you mean?"

49

"No, of course not. Nothing as good as this." Marvin nudges his now-empty plate away, a tiny movement with just one finger. "Then we heard a child crying, so we looked around. And there she was. A little girl was sitting at a nearby table all alone. Lesley asked where her parents were, and she told us she was lost."

Ruth is cradling the baby monitor in her lap. It lies there uselessly, the cord drooping.

"I thought about leaving her with the security guard on patrol," he goes on, "but he looked like a creep. So Lesley took one of her hands and I took the other, and we walked all around the mall until we found her mom and dad. And do you know what they were doing?" He glances around the table. "Take a guess."

Haltingly, Ruth asks, "Looking for her?"

Marvin shakes his head. "They were shopping. They didn't even know she was gone."

Stef dips a finger into the thin, red pool on her plate. Her mouth is a straight line. "What were they buying?"

"Shoes. A pair for each of them." He smiles tightly and gulps his wine.

"Did they say thank you?" says Ruth. "To you and your wife?"

Sammy raises an eyebrow at her. "That's a funny question."

She stares back at him. "Why?"

Stef shuffles closer to her husband, and he puts his arm around her when she says, "Because of course they would."

"You'd think that," says Marvin. "But the answer is no." He goes back to his wine, and the story is over.

Ruth scans around for an outlet and sees one on the wall beside her. She plugs in the little white box and sets it on the table, and the room immediately fills with the muffled noises from the movie downstairs.

Stef frowns at it. "Why'd you bring that up here?"

"In case something happens," says Ruth.

Stef tilts her head. "What could happen?"

"Anything," says Marvin.

As if on cue, a staticky squeal blares from the monitor, and Ruth jolts and knocks over her wine glass.

In a flurry of motion it breaks into pieces on the table and Stef rolls her eyes and says, "You're a liability, woman," and moves to sweep the shards into her hand—*Why would she do that? It's not safe*, Ruth thinks—and then Stef yelps and yanks her hand back and sticks her thumb in her mouth, and when she pulls it out again there is blood on her lips.

"Babe," Sammy says, "you cut yourself."

"Shit," says Stef. "Does somebody have a Band-Aid?"

"I've got some in the backpack," says Ruth.

Stef flashes a gory grin. "Of course you do."

Ruth gets up and goes to the living room, where the backpack waits in a corner.

An image appears in her mind: nine-year-old Stef sitting on Ruth's mother's lap in a hospital waiting room, holding her bandaged hand and squeezing tears out of the corners of her eyes. Stef had cut herself on glass back at their house and had a wide gash across her palm. She only did it for attention and now she was getting it so she was happy, not sad. Ruth could tell they weren't real tears.

The waiting room was full and Ruth's dad was sitting across from them, reading a magazine. Every so often he'd glance up at Ruth, in her chair next to her mom and Stef, and smile, and she'd smile back but only if Stef wasn't watching.

51

The girls had been playing in the family room while Ruth's parents were upstairs, and then Stef was mean and broke something like she always did.

"Does it still hurt?" Ruth's mom asked Stef, and Stef nodded and made pathetic kitten sounds and cuddled in closer.

On the mint-green wall above their heads was a framed photograph of a wide-open field under fluffy, white clouds. Ruth sat on her hard, wooden waiting-room chair and stared at it. She wanted to climb into the picture and run across the grass and disappear into the trees that she knew were there, just outside the frame.

Ruth's dad put down his magazine and stood up. "Ruthie, let's go get some snacks."

"Okay." She jumped up, hiding her grin as she followed him out of the room.

"I want a Kit Kat!" Stef yelled after them, and then they were free.

The hallway outside extended infinitely in either direction. Ruth squinted but she couldn't see the end anywhere.

"It's a maze," her dad said. "And there's the treasure."

He pointed at the vending machine to their right and Ruth ran over.

There were rows of red-and-yellow packages on top and rows of blue-and-green packages on the bottom. Someone must have arranged them that way, to look nice. Soothing colours in a sad place. By squeezing her eyes half shut, she could almost fool herself into thinking she was gazing at the sun setting over a lake. But only if she concentrated really hard.

"Did Stef break the photo on purpose?" her dad asked from way up above her.

She leaned forward and a small circle of the vending-machine window fogged up with her breath.

Stef had dangled a glass-framed photograph of Ruth and her parents, all three of them smiling, over the tiles on the edge of the family room. "Oh no," she said, "this is very slippery."

"Don't!" said Ruth.

Stef frowned. "Do you actually think I would?" And then she dropped it and it smashed, and her mouth and her eyes went round with shock.

Ruth's eyes widened too. "Now you're in trouble."

Stef knelt down and started picking up the pieces and sliced her hand almost immediately. "I think I need a Band-Aid," she said numbly, and started to cry.

Behind the blur of condensation, all the colours in the vending machine bled together—red and yellow and blue and green. "No," Ruth told her dad without looking at him. Even though she could've said yes, and he would've believed her. "It was an accident."

"Okay." He squeezed her shoulder. "She wanted a Kit Kat, right? What about you?"

She shook her head and reached up to rub the window so it was clear again. So that anyone passing by, with their own reasons to be sad, could get exactly what they wanted.

Ruth finds a Band-Aid in the backpack for Stef, who has followed her into the living room, and gives it to her. The cut is minor this time, skimming across the faded scar on Stef's palm from her long-ago stitches.

"Thanks," says Stef.

"Don't mention it," says Ruth, and they walk back to the screened porch, where Marvin and Sammy are arguing about something.

Both men's voices are raised and Stef says, "Whoa, whoa!" as she slides back onto the picnic bench next to Sammy, whose face is ruddy and tense. "What's going on here?"

Marvin grits his teeth, waving a dismissive hand at Sammy. "He doesn't get it."

Ruth hovers in the doorway, then takes a few tentative steps into the room. "Doesn't get what?"

"That it's not something to joke about."

"We don't know what you're talking about." Stef keeps her voice light, enunciating the words to make them sound goofy. Trying and failing to defuse the hostility that thickens the air.

54

"All I *said* was, 'Everybody needs a break once in a while.'" Sammy crosses his arms. "I was merely observing—humor-ously—that those parents in the mall picked a good day to abandon their child. *Because Marvin and Lesley were there.*" He shakes his head at Marvin. "I was giving you a compliment."

Marvin is trembling with anger now, but manages to keep his tone level. "And *then* you said I don't have kids so I wouldn't understand."

Sammy throws up his hands. "But you don't! And that wasn't a dig! I am envious of you and your carefree lifestyle!"

"Jesus, Sammy," says Stef. "Back off, okay? The guy's upset."

Ruth's back is flat against the wall. She pushes harder but there's nowhere else to go.

Marvin blows out a long breath. "Those people don't deserve that little girl."

The baby monitor crackles to life then, and a child's disem-bodied voice bellows, "Mommmmyyyyy! It's oooover!"

The wail echoes around the room, and all of the adults turn toward the source of it.

"Shut that thing up, will you?" Stef says to Ruth, who nods.

"I think that was Fern," she says, mostly to herself, as she hurries to the outlet.

"I'll do it." Marvin reaches over, unplugs the monitor and gently bundles it up with the cord. He hands it to Ruth with a gallant flourish. "For you." Then he stands up unsteadily and announces, "Time to go home."

On the other side of the screen, the night has erased everything. Lake, trees, sky—they're all gone.

Hesitantly, Ruth asks him, "How are you getting there?"

Marvin wobbles as he climbs over the picnic bench. "Same way I came in."

Ruth glances at Stef and Sammy, who don't seem concerned. "I don't think you should be on the water now, though. It's pretty dark out there."

"Don't worry." He reaches into his shorts pocket and produces a small, silver light attached to a strap. "I've got my trusty headlamp."

"What about a life jacket?" she asks.

"Marvin goes night paddling all the time," Stef tells her. "He'll be fine."

"Maybe we should call Lesley and let her know you're on your way?" Ruth suggests.

Marvin shakes his head. "She'll be fast asleep by now."

"Lesley's not much of a partier," Stef adds. "That's why Marvin likes to hang out with us. At least, until my husband starts acting like an asshole. *Say sorry*," she orders Sammy through clenched teeth.

"Sorry, Marvin," Sammy mumbles. "Are we still good?"

"Always." Marvin's expression clears and he beams around at all of them, then raises a hand to his forehead in a crisp salute and opens the screen door. "Goodnight, chums."

"See you tomorrow, buddy," says Sammy.

"Are you sure you're going to be all right?" Ruth calls after him, but then he's gone.

"Awww," says Stef. "You two are adorable."

Ruth frowns. "I'm going to put Fern to bed," she says, and heads to the basement.

ALL THREE GIRLS are using the couch as a trampoline when Ruth walks into the playroom. "Bedtime, honey," she tells Fern, and picks her up and hauls her away.

Fern struggles in her arms and her voice rings with outrage when she protests, "Not yet! Not yet!"

"Leave her alone!" Amelia yells.

"Yeah!" Isabelle shouts. "We were having fun!"

"I think it's your bedtime too," Ruth tells them, but they ignore her and keep bouncing, their long hair whipping around them.

Carrying Fern, Ruth tosses the monitor receiver onto her own bed to plug in later, grabs an overnight pull-up from Fern's room, then heads to the bathroom. When they're inside and the door is closed, Ruth sets her daughter down and says, "Now let's get your pull-up on and brush your teeth."

Fern is fuming now. Her little face is red and her lips are pressed tightly together. She shakes her head.

Ruth sighs. "We have to get ready for bed, sweetie. It's late."

"No."

"Fine, then I'll help you." Ruth squeezes a thin line of fluoride-free training toothpaste onto Fern's toothbrush, which is purple and shaped like a stegosaurus. "Open up," she says, and when she pushes the brush into Fern's mouth, the plastic spikes on the dinosaur's tail dig into Ruth's palm.

She scrubs the top teeth as thoroughly as she can, but Fern closes her lips around the brush before the bottom teeth are done. Ruth hesitates, but persists when she imagines the little molars swimming in sugar, rotting from the outside in. She tries to be careful, but Fern gags anyway.

"I'm sorry, honey." Ruth lets out a shaky sigh as she rinses the brush in the sink. "Okay, let's get your pull-up on. Do you want to have a pee on the toilet first?"

Fern doesn't move. Her small hands are balled into fists and her little voice vibrates with wrath. "I hate you."

Ruth sucks in a breath. "What?"

Fern has never said those words before but now she says them again, louder this time.

"Please don't say that," says Ruth. "I'm just trying to help."

"I can do it myself!" Fern yanks off her pyjama pants and underwear, yanks on the pull-up, then shoves past Ruth to open the door and stomp to her bedroom.

Ruth follows behind, tensed for the next barrage. But when she steps through the doorway, her daughter is already in bed, smiling brightly at her.

"Hi, Mama! Can you read me stories now?"

Ruth exhales and sits down heavily, all of her strength draining away. "I would love to." She tucks the blanket up around Fern's neck, then frowns at the stubborn orange crust still glued to one corner of her mouth.

She licks her thumb and scrubs at it, making Fern yelp, "Too hard, Mama!"

"Sorry." Ruth folds her hands into her lap, chastened. "You had some sauce on your mouth."

"Mmm." Fern's voice goes dreamy. "That was good pasta."

"You know that wasn't real cheese, right?"

Fern's eyes widen. "What was it?"

Ruth leans close and whispers in her daughter's seashell ear, "*Alien* cheese."

Fern smiles. "Silly Mommy."

Ruth switches on the night light she'd packed, checks that the monitor transmitter is still on, tucks her trusty pair of foam safety bumpers securely in place under the fitted sheet on either side of the mattress so Fern can't accidentally roll onto the floor in the middle of the night and snuggles Monsieur Foomay up under her sleepy child's arm.

The plush dragon with his shiny scales and wings is Fern's favourite toy, and she used to tote him around with her everywhere. Now she mostly just needs him at night, but she still expects Ruth to be aware of his location at all times.

Stef gave him to Ruth as a baby-shower gift, even though there was no baby shower. Ruth said it wasn't something she wanted.

She couldn't picture herself at the centre of a room full of streamers and balloons, playing those stupid games where you had to wear a safety pin with a tiny diaper on it, and if you crossed your legs or said the word *baby*, then you lost your safety pin. She didn't want her mom and James's mom to collect the ribbons and bows from all the gifts and attach them to a paper plate to make a bonnet that Ruth would have to wear for the rest of the day, just to prove she was going to be a mother herself soon. Even though their moms would've liked that.

But Stef gave Ruth the dragon anyway. James brought the present home from work, along with a card with a cartoon stork on the front. A pastel-pink bundle dangled from its sharp beak, and on the inside Stef had written, "From your knight in shining armour."

Ruth had held the soft toy in her lap as the wrapping paper

drifted to the floor. She stared at her friend's words in the card until they blurred. "What does that mean?"

"Nothing," said James. "It doesn't mean anything. She's just joking."

"Why are you looking at me so hard?" says Fern. "Is there more sauce on me?"

Ruth shakes her head and smooths out the blanket on either side of her daughter. "What did you think of the movie? Was it good?"

"It was about a princess," says Fern.

"Yes, in a bog, right?"

"What's a bog?"

"Like a swamp."

"Oh."

Outside the thin, rattling glass of Fern's window, the wind makes a cartoon *Woo!* noise over and over again.

"Was it funny like *Puppy Commander*?"

"Nope."

"It wasn't funny? What happened in it?"

Fern clutches at Ruth's arm. "She went in the water and she died."

Ruth thinks, *Fuck.* She says, "Really?"

"The creatures got her. They made her go in the water and then she died and she grew a tail like a fish and she had a black hoodie on so I couldn't see her face."

Ruth looks at the night outside the window.

Fern says, "It's darker here than at home."

"Yes, it is."

"I want to go home."

"Soon," Ruth tells her. "We're going to stay here for a while and have lots of fun first."

"I don't want to stay here." Fern starts to cry.

Ruth grapples with her impatient sigh before it wrenches free and fills the room. She almost says, *Me neither*, but instead she asks, "How about I read you extra stories tonight?"

The sobs slow to sniffles and Fern cuddles closer. "Okay, Mama."

THERE IS A voicemail on Ruth's phone and she doesn't want to listen to it.

Her mother's voice will be sad and that will make Ruth sad too. The notification sits there blinking at her, but she doesn't press the button that will summon the gentle robot voice that will lead her to her mother's message. She'll listen to it later.

Ruth lies next to Fern, who's asleep now, and imagines strong arms around her, and a deep voice hushed and full of love.

Then she sighs and sets her phone to Do Not Disturb. It's too late to call her mom back anyway.

The cottage is quiet and Ruth wonders if Stef and Sammy are still in the living room or if they've gone up to bed. She hopes they've gone up to bed.

She eases herself off the mattress, careful not to wake her snoring daughter. She takes her phone and tiptoes to the door and cringes when it creaks open. She throws an anxious glance over her shoulder but Fern hasn't moved. She closes the door and steps into the dark playroom.

She stands very still and listens for noise from upstairs, but hears nothing. She climbs the stairs slowly. At the top, she inches the door open and peeks through the crack. The main floor is silent, and dimly illuminated by the stove light.

Ruth is surprised because it's late, but still early for Stef. It doesn't matter, though. She's glad for the break. She hurries to the screen door and frowns when she sees it's unlocked. *Do they always leave it unlocked at night?*

She slips on her sandals and slides the door open. She steps outside and closes the door and she's alone, she's alone, and she takes a deep breath of the cool, fresh, piney air that smells like Christmas.

Then she shivers a little. She should've brought a sweater, but if she goes back inside to get one, she might wake someone up. She'll tolerate being cold.

She starts down the steep staircase to the beach and realizes she also should've brought a flashlight because the night is pitch-black. But she'll manage. She grips the railing and makes her way to the bottom, and when she finally steps onto the sand, there is the moon, nearly full, shining on the lake. And the dock.

When she gets there, she walks to the end and sits down on the rough wood and lies back, cradling her head in her folded arms, and looks up at the stars.

All around her, the crickets and the frogs are singing. Every so often there is a small splash nearby, and sometimes a big one. There are other sounds too, harder to identify and potentially more ominous. Furtive rustling and snuffling from somewhere in the woods. Twigs snapping.

But she isn't worried. She's here alone and the stars and the moon are so bright, and her dad's voice is rumbling in her ear again, giving names to all of the constellations.

Then, before she can stop them, her thoughts fly away to just a few years ago, when he was gone. Her father was dead, and the sandwiches at his funeral were crustless and very small.

She'd lifted an egg-salad one from the silver tray on the long table in the middle of the crowded reception room and pinched it between her thumb and forefinger, and the yellow filling squished out the sides and onto an upturned hand that was suddenly there.

"Yum," said Stef, "I love it when they make them with chives." She licked the mess off her palm and winked.

"I'll get you a napkin," said Ruth.

"Don't worry about it," Stef told her. "You have enough on your plate today."

62

"A plate." Ruth said the word like she was trying it out for the first time. "Can you get me one?"

"Yes," said Stef. "I can definitely do that." She picked one off the pile and frowned at it. "It's empty, though. I can't give it to you empty."

Ruth stared at all the food laid out in front of them. "I don't know what I want."

"Of course you don't. Let me help you out." Stef started loading up the plate even though Ruth wasn't even hungry, but Ruth didn't tell her stop.

At the far end of the room, her sad mother raised her pale hand and fluttered her fingers in a wave, and Ruth repeated the motions back to her.

"How's she doing?" Stef asked.

"As well as possible, I guess." Ruth shrugged. "Not good."

Stef pushed the plate with its mountain of miniature sandwiches and desserts toward Ruth, but Ruth shook her head.

"I don't think my mom would care if my dad died." Stef plucked a lemon square off the plate and shoved it into her wide-open mouth, then mumbled, "That was a completely unnecessary and thoughtless thing to say, I'm sorry."

"It's okay." The collar of Ruth's new black dress was too tight, and she tugged at it. She had gone to the mall immediately after her mom called with the news. She didn't cry, she just went shopping. Because the only thought in her head was, *I need a black dress. I don't have any black dresses and I need one now.* So she went and bought the dress without trying it on, and now she could see that was a mistake.

Stef looked left and right. "Where's James?"

"He had to take a call. He didn't want to leave but I said it was fine. He'll be back soon."

"Are you serious?" Stef tossed the plate onto the table, spilling food onto the floor, and yanked her phone from the back pocket of her slim black pants. She hammered out a message and punched Send. "I told him to forget about work today. He's on his way back. Now get over here and give me a hug while you're waiting."

Ruth moved into her friend's embrace. "How are the twins?" she asked against Stef's shoulder.

"Hell if I know. They're assholes, I can tell you that much. Terrible twos all the way. Amelia has started vomiting out of spite. And when I said goodbye this morning, Isabelle took off her diaper and threw it at me. Fortunately, it was only full of pee this time. Anyway, Sammy's got them today, so lucky him. I'm just glad for the break."

Ruth tensed at that and pulled away, but Stef wouldn't let her go. She just held on tighter. "Jesus, I'm an idiot. Just ignore me, all right?"

Ruth nodded and tried to smile, and the two of them stood there together under the high ceiling with the fluorescent light beating down.

Every so often, random mourners would pass by and nod at

Ruth. Their smiles were tentative and respectful but they never said anything.

"I'm sorry we weren't around when it happened," Stef whispered in Ruth's ear.

"I know," she whispered back. "It's okay."

Even with Stef's arms wrapped around her, Ruth was freezing. The air conditioning was too cold and there were Kleenex boxes on every available surface, and she imagined taking all the tissues out and weaving them into a blanket that she would climb under and never leave. She should've bought a new cardigan to wear with her new dress, but she didn't.

"What are you doing out here all alone, loser?"

And here is her friend, appearing out of the darkness with a bottle of wine. Bounding across the dock and making it bounce, making ripples and then waves grow in the lake, forcing the wood and the water to accommodate her and her giant grin, which glows at Ruth as it gets closer and closer and then it's gone, and Stef lays a heavy hand on Ruth's shoulder and says in a low, urgent whisper, "We need to get naked immediately."

"What?" says Ruth.

"Our children are asleep. And Sammy just told me he was really tired and he did this big, fake yawn and kissed me goodnight and said I should stay up if I wanted to, which means he's looking at porn on his laptop under the covers right now so he'll be occupied for a while. And your husband isn't here. Which means you and I must go skinny-dipping right fucking now."

"I don't know. I'm pretty tired." Ruth yawns widely, then covers her mouth when Stef raises an eyebrow. "I was just about to head back up to the cottage."

"No, you weren't. Liar. You were going to keep sitting here, lost in your sad, sappy thoughts, until I rescued you. Which is what I'm trying to do at this very moment, if you'll stop being so stubborn and just take off all your clothes."

Ruth doesn't move.

"Here, hold this." Stef reaches down to give Ruth the wine bottle, and then her fingers fly up to the waistband of her loose pants. She undoes the drawstring and lets them fall. "What are you waiting for? Take a swig and do what I'm doing."

She makes it sound and look so easy. She peels off her T-shirt next, and the skin underneath is smooth and firm.

Ruth is sitting cross-legged on the dock and she can feel where her soft belly bulges out over the waistband of her jeans. She has always hated waistbands.

"Come on, chicken." Stef stands before her in her bra and underwear. Then she takes those off too, turns around and dives gracefully into the lake with barely a splash.

And Ruth stares at her, like she always does. Awed by all the things her friend's body can do. How capable it is.

Stef surfaces, her long hair slick against her head, and smiles. "Have another drink," she says. "You'll feel better."

So she does. Then another. Then one more before she puts the bottle down and stands up.

"Now strip."

So she does.

"Look at you," Stef says when Ruth's clothes are in a heap at her feet. "Gorgeous lady."

Ruth shakes her head. "No, I'm not."

"Oh, get over yourself and take a fucking compliment. You better keep that negative self-talk to yourself, Ruthie, or else you'll give Fern a complex."

She bristles. "I never talk like that in front of Fern."

"Good. And I don't want to hear it, either."

Ruth breathes away her anger because she knows there is a purpose to this. This is what they do. Stef teases and Ruth bristles and then they both start laughing because it's all so ridiculous, this pattern they repeat. The motions they go through together, always together, no matter what.

She closes her eyes and plugs her nose and jumps into the water.

And it's wonderful. She is free and wild and not even too cold! She breaks the surface and opens her eyes, grinning, ready to admit, *Okay fine, this was a good idea.*

But Stef is nowhere to be seen.

Ruth looks all around. The moonlit lake is still and there are no sounds.

"Stef!"

Nothing.

It's deeper off the dock than she'd expected. Her toes can barely touch the bottom. She treads water with her heart beating fast.

During the day, the water was clear and she could see all the way down. Now it's black and she can't see anything. Her invisible feet kick beneath her.

More time passes. *Where the fuck is Stef?* Something brushes against her leg and she flinches away. Big fish with sharp teeth could be circling her right now. Anything could be in the water with her.

She'd forgotten about the bloodstained pad in her underwear when she took it off, but she remembers it now. She remembers a room filled with that red metallic smell, heavy and warm and slightly sweet. She imagines the air and the water filling with it now. What that would attract.

"Stef!"

Still no answer.

Her friend is gone and she's alone in black water by a black forest with a black sky pressing down.

Something catches her eye, far off to the left. A lonely light, glinting. Bobbing up and down, gliding along.

He left a while ago, she thinks. *That can't be him.*

She blinks and the light disappears. Just the moon reflecting off the lake. That's all it was.

There's a distant splash then, and laughter. "I'm over here!" Stef shouts from far away.

Ruth releases the breath she was holding, the force of the exhale propelling her down. She kicks back up and calls out, "Okay!" Forcing a lighthearted tone and refusing to admit she was worried.

Stef swims over with strong, confident strokes, getting closer and closer.

Ruth imagines Marvin getting home and slipping quietly into bed next to his sleeping wife. She wonders if James is asleep now, or awake. What he's doing alone in the dark.

Just a few feet away now, Stef ducks under again. A moment later she resurfaces right beside Ruth and splashes her in the face. "Wake up," she says. "The night is young."

Ruth retaliates with a quick flick of her wrist and Stef sputters under the spray, and they both laugh.

Stef paddles over to the dock and retrieves the bottle of wine. She takes a big glug and passes it to Ruth.

Ruth takes a long drink and sets the bottle on the dock. Then she lets her legs drift up so she's floating on her back and gazing at the big, round moon. "This is pretty nice, actually."

Her friend grins. "What did I tell you?" Then she takes a deep, loud breath, and disappears again.

. . . .

In the middle of the night, Ruth wakes up and James is there.

She stares at the wall in the dark and listens to his breathing, feels his warmth on the bed behind her.

She could roll over and wrap an arm around him, rest her hand on his chest right over his heartbeat. But it sounds like he's fast asleep, so she decides to keep her eyes closed too.

She lies there and smiles and thinks about how good they are together. They're great, actually.

For the longest time, she used to worry that they weren't. If she sensed any distance between them, she was sure that was the end. Or she'd say something and he wouldn't respond the way she expected and she'd think, *He doesn't want to be with me anymore.*

But eventually she started to relax. She believed him, most of the time, when he told her he loved her. And then she'd catch him looking at her with a weird expression on his face, and for the rest of the day, she'd wait for him to tell her that he'd chosen someone else.

The first time they kissed was the first time they met. In Stef's dorm room, sitting together on Stef's single bed. They'd been drinking, but not a lot. Stef had taken her little battery-powered boom box into the hallway to start a dance party, and suddenly Ruth and James were alone and he was giving her a big, goofy grin. Stef's old stuffed cat, the one she'd brought to every sleepover at Ruth's house when they were kids, was lying between them, grey and mangy and deflated. Ruth picked it up and tossed it on the floor.

James said, "Hello, there," and leaned in closer.

Ruth said, "What about Stef?"

He shrugged. "She's like my sister. Or at least what I imagine a sister would be like. Different from you, anyway."

Ruth smiled at that and leaned in too.

Then Stef walked back into her room and they sprang apart. "What just happened here?" she said, and at the same time they answered, "Nothing." And they all laughed.

Stef ran back out to the hallway and returned with Sammy on her arm, and then they were four.

Except, Ruth knew, that wasn't the way it was supposed to go. Stef was supposed to get the cute one, like always, and Ruth should've ended up with the pudgy, prematurely balding dork eating onion pizza and voguing to Pearl Jam out in the hall.

After a while, she falls back asleep and dreams about another man in another room who gives her a kiss. That's all it is, just a kiss, but it tastes bad. And Stef thinks it's hilarious.

"Mama?"

Ruth wakes up and James isn't there. Of course he isn't.

"Shh," she tells her daughter, "go back to sleep."

"I woke up and you weren't here," Fern murmurs in Ruth's ear. "I had a bad dream."

"I'm sorry, honey. I'm here now."

They're in Fern's room, in the basement of Stef and Sammy's cottage. And James is in their new home, without them.

Fern burrows under the covers and curls against her, and Ruth wriggles closer and inhales her daughter's stinky-sweet breath.

The bed is basically a crib, the way Ruth has set it up, with the safety rails tucked under the fitted sheet on either side of them.

She misses the way Fern would gaze up from her real crib in their old apartment, her chubby baby arms reaching and fingers wiggling. *You're the one I want. Nobody else.* She was safe in there too, always content to wait for Ruth or James to lift her

69

out. Stef used to joke that the twins kept escaping from their cage, but Fern never even tried to climb out of hers.

Now she has a "big-girl bed" at home with pink polka-dot sheets that she picked out for herself. And eventually the safety rails will be put away, and they won't need to travel with them either. They probably don't need to travel with them now, but Ruth feels better knowing they're in place.

The two of them lie there tangled up together and Fern drifts off, her chest and belly moving up and down.

Sometimes Ruth has to focus really hard on those parts of the little body when she looks in on Fern at night, because she can't immediately detect that reassuring rise and fall. She'll stand there watching, watching, until she sees it.

Not long after Fern was born, Stef told her, "Just so you know, sometimes when she's sleeping and you go in to check on her, she might look like she isn't breathing at first. She'll be lying there so completely still, not moving at all, and you will be sure she's dead. And your first instinct will be to poke her and prod her, anything to get a reaction that will reassure you she's okay. But here's what you do: smother that instinct and wait ten seconds instead."

"What the hell, are you kidding me?" said Ruth. "Why would I wait?"

"Because if you just stand there and slowly count to ten, I guarantee you that she will move in that time. An eyelash flutter, a finger flick, something. Trust me on this. Because if something is wrong, which it won't be, then waiting ten seconds cannot possibly make it worse. But if everything is fine, which it will be, you can relax—and the best news is, she'll still be asleep!"

"No," Ruth had said, "the best news is she'll still be alive."

"Right, yes," said Stef. "That too."

Ruth is in Fern's bed now because of the nightmares.

Earlier she'd woken in her own bedroom to Fern's screams, high and terrified, amplified a million times on the monitor.

Ruth half fell out of bed, ice in her spine, fumbling in the unfamiliar dark for the doorknob and shaking her head. *Fucking Bog Princess*.

The monitor vibrated again with her daughter's distorted fear, the staticky shriek like a funhouse sound effect blaring from a speaker inside a dangling skeleton with red eyes.

She walked into the hall and stood outside Fern's door, waiting for the next scream. But there was only silence. She hesitated before going in. If Fern had fallen back to sleep, she didn't want to wake her up again.

One night a long time ago, when Ruth was just a couple years older than Fern, she'd woken up and Stef wasn't there. She'd been sleeping beside Ruth and then she wasn't, and for a while Ruth lay alone in her bed, happy to have it to herself again with only Stef's stuffed cat for company. Stef always hogged the blankets so Ruth pulled all of them around her, but then she was too warm. She threw them off and climbed out of bed, wondering where her friend had gone.

She stood in the middle of her room, listening for clues. But there was only quiet. She took a deep breath, walked to her door and opened it.

The hallway was darker because there was no night light. At the end of it, though, was her parents' bedroom, and if she moved quickly, she could get there before anything got her.

Her small shadow followed her along the wall, keeping pace with her until she reached her parents' door, which was open just a crack. She put her hand on it and pushed, and it creaked open.

And there they were. It was still so dark, but her night-animal eyes could see. Her mom and dad were sleeping on either side of their big bed, with a smaller form nestled between them.

Ruth had stood there, alone on the carpet, small hands balling into fists at her sides. Listening to the three of them breathing softly together.

Ruth opened Fern's door and stepped in. The room was quiet.

"Mommy?" The word came out in a whisper. Fern was cowering under her blankets, staring at her. "I thought you were a monster."

"Oh, honey, I'm sorry. I thought you were sleeping." Ruth crawled into bed with Fern and curled around her. "But there's no such thing as monsters, remember?"

Fern twisted away and fixed her with wide, searching eyes. "Then why are you scared too?"

THREE

THE WIFE SITS IN THE TIKI BAR A FEW BLOCKS AWAY FROM her apartment and feels happier because it's very tropical. Lots of rattan and bamboo. The servers are wearing hula skirts and the bartender is wearing a lei.

A plastic flamingo hangs from the ceiling. The walls and the floor are painted yellow and green and pink and purple and blue. The stereo is playing Polynesian jazz and the TV over the bar is playing *Hawaii Five*-O on mute.

The situation is unfolding the way it's supposed to: the husband is on his island and the wife is on hers.

She shifts her weight on her stool. Underneath her tight clothes she's wearing a bulky maxi-pad, and she's going to have to change it soon. She looks at the stack of parrot-and-palm-tree-patterned cocktail napkins on the bar and thinks, *Are those things sanitary?* She laughs at her own silly joke.

The stool has a back and arms, so it's a high chair. (She laughs again.) She likes the view it gives her. She's up above the crowd so she can see things more clearly. She can see all the way to another part of the world if she wants to.

In the centre of the dance floor, a giant rainbow-hued disco ball turns and turns, and the wife shields her eyes against the flashing light to peer at the shapes of couples swaying together. She looks toward them but instead she sees the resort where her husband and her best friend are right now, without her. Which she can't actually see, of course, but she can imagine it so well. She can imagine them.

"It's for work!" her husband said before he left her alone. "It's just another boring work trip."

That's why the wife wasn't invited. That's why she's here and they're there.

The miscarriage was even earlier this time too, so her husband wasn't worried about her. She'd only just found out she was pregnant before she felt the familiar pinch at the small of her back and the warmth gathering between her legs. She wasn't even surprised when it happened. She was expecting it.

But she was still bleeding, and he left anyway.

"The doctor said you're fine, didn't she?" He gave her a kiss and then he packed his suitcase.

The wife and the husband went to a resort once, for their honeymoon. Way back at the beginning, before they ever tried to have a baby, when everything was easier.

First they met and then they fell in love. They used to smoke way too much pot and climb onto rooftops and look across the whole city together and pretend it was all theirs. They used to go to concerts and he'd hold her and she'd lean against him and they'd sway together in the dark. She was his favourite person and he was her fellow adventurer, her knight in digital armour who could fix any problem with a single click.

Even when it was just the two of them, though, her friend was always there.

Even when the wife was a child, and her parents rented a cottage for two weeks every summer and that was the only time when it was just the three of them, her friend was always there, taking up too much room in everyone's minds.

She has always been there.

And the wife has always been fine.

Even their fertility doctor said it. She sat in her sunny office in the bright, sterile clinic with its unsmiling nurses and white walls and futuristic chrome furniture and told the wife, "We can't find anything wrong with you. All of your tests have been inconclusive. There's really no reason why you shouldn't be able to carry a healthy baby to full term." Those words were in her chart, so they had to mean something.

The wife finishes up her fourth cocktail. This one was a mai tai. She can't remember the names of the other three but they were equally sweet, and she loved them all. Four is a nice, round number, so maybe she'll stop now. Or maybe not. She raises her nearly empty glass in a toast. *To you*, she thinks, *whoever you are*.

One summer at the cottage with her parents, she built a clam zoo. Her father had been diving down deep and collecting clams for her all day, so she needed a place to keep them safe.

She started by stacking rocks in a circle in the shallow part of the water next to the sand, which was as close to the lake as she was allowed to be. She kept stacking rocks until the walls were high enough so none of the clams could escape. But then one did.

She studied the clam sitting there in its boring, brown shell. So bad to be out of its cage. She was alone on the beach and her parents were far away, and she decided to smash it.

She picked up the clam and threw it down hard on a rock, but the shell was too strong and it just bounced off. She picked it up again and threw it down harder, and this time, a tiny crack appeared. Then she remembered that the clam was out of the zoo because she took it out. So it wasn't the clam's fault but never mind because *too late, too late.*

She was a seagull and the clam was her food and she wanted to eat it, so she hurled it at the rocks again and then the shell split open completely. There was the oozing, white body. There was the broken brown shell. But there was no blood. *Where did all the blood go?* It was white inside, and when she knelt down and examined it more closely, she saw a rainbow.

She gathered up the pieces of broken shell and the squiggly, slimy guts and held them against her cheek and then her skin was slimy too but she didn't care. Overhead, the real gulls were circling, screaming at her to get out of the way, give it to them, they were so very hungry, but she told them no.

She ran and ran and was out of breath when she reached the cottage. She had no voice and she couldn't shout for her dad but then he was there anyway. He banged out the screen door and rushed over and knelt down and pulled her into a hug. "What's wrong? Tell me what's wrong." So she told him about the clam and she showed him too, but he wasn't even mad. He said he could tell she was sorry but why did she do it?

She dropped the pieces of shell on the grass and wiped the wetness from the guts onto her shorts. "I never want her to come here, ever," she told him. And he said, "Don't worry, honey, she won't. This is our place. It's only for us."

And then he appears.

A thin man with thinning hair and a Hawaiian shirt, gliding toward her through a sea of men wearing Hawaiian shirts, so it almost looks like he can disappear and reappear at will. Almost.

He grins at her and calls out, "Aloha!"

She looks to her left and right. There's nobody here but her, but she still doesn't believe she's the one he wants.

When she was little, her friend used to dare her to follow strange men into public washrooms. "Go in there and tell him you love him," she'd say. "Maybe he wants to marry you."

The stranger comes closer. He asks if he can buy her a drink, and she says yes.

He pays for a rum punch, which comes in half a coconut, and presents it to her.

"Thank you," she says, and takes a sip. It's very sweet.

"Now," he says, "what are you going to give me for it?"

She doesn't answer. Just cradles the broken shell and peeks inside. When she moves even slightly, the tiniest waves appear.

FOUR

In the morning, Sammy shovels up a load of scrambled eggs and pronounces, with his mouth full, "Statistically, the world is a lot safer now than when we were kids."

Ruth is working on a bowl of cornflakes, which do not look appealing at all. The cereal is bloated with lukewarm milk and slowly disintegrating, particles breaking away to form a layer of scum on the surface.

She and Stef and Sammy are sitting around the kitchen table. Outside on the deck, Fern is watching Amelia and Isabelle take turns skipping. Every so often they give her a chance to try, and she gets tangled in the rope and all three of them laugh uncontrollably.

Ruth rubs her sticky, stinging eyes and cradles her pounding head. She'd stayed awake in her bed for a long time after their swim, with her hands resting on her belly. The cramps had stopped a while ago, but the blood just kept coming. Keeping her company.

Eventually she'd drifted off, lulled by the peaceful static from the baby-monitor receiver standing at attention on her bedside table, until Fern started screaming.

They use the same monitor at home, so they can always hear Fern if she calls for them. Sometimes Ruth lies awake at night listening to the static, and occasionally Fern will mumble in her sleep—nonsense words strung together in a sentence—and Ruth will wonder what she's dreaming about.

Once, what feels like a long time ago but wasn't really, she lay in bed at their old apartment and listened to James's voice on the monitor telling Fern the magical story of how she came to them. Fern didn't ask any questions at the end. She just said, "Okay," and went to sleep. And they never talked about it again.

Ruth reaches for her coffee and takes a scalding sip, then carefully puts the mug back down. There's a cartoon on it, showing a bear and a moose sitting at a bar. The moose has tire tracks criss-crossing his body and one of his antlers is cracking off, and he's saying to the bear, "You should see the other guy."

She asks Sammy, "Where did you find your statistics?"

"Places." He lifts a random section from the weekend paper and waves it at her. "Sure, sometimes somebody digs up a suitcase full of tiny bones. That happens."

"Holy shit, Sammy." Stef shakes her head at him, but she's smiling. "You are the worst human being."

"But it's not happening *more* now, is what I'm saying. It's always happened. So why do we talk about it more now? Because the Bad Stranger is our boogeyman. Way more kids die every day from drowning or falling down the stairs or choking on hot dogs. But nobody talks about that. It's more exciting to swap urban legends about this or that little boy or girl getting scooped into a van and never being seen again."

"Mama!"

Ruth jumps up. "Fern?" She pivots toward her daughter's anxious voice. "Are you okay?"

Fern squishes her happy face up against the screen. "Where's Monsieur Foomay?"

Exhale. *She's fine.* "He's in the backpack."

The backpack is ever-present, always stocked with an extra pair of pants and underwear in case Fern has a rare accident, an extra shirt in case she spills something disgusting on herself, a spare plastic bag to potentially contain either the potentially wet pants and underwear or the potentially gross shirt, extra socks in case Fern's feet get cold or the socks she's wearing get wet somehow, pull-ups and a back-up pair of pyjamas in case they go somewhere and stay out late, first-aid supplies, extra toothbrush, wet wipes, snacks and a sippy cup, storybooks and sticker books and colouring books and crayons and, of course— when he's not with Fern—Monsieur Foomay.

"Thanks, Mama!"

Laughter from the twins. The word *baby* muffled by matching sets of hands.

Ruth sits back down.

She never minds bringing the backpack everywhere because Fern has her own loads to carry. Whenever Ruth empties out her daughter's pockets, she finds rocks, twigs, old elastics, lost buttons, scraps of dirty ribbon. She found a small coil of snakeskin once, papery thin, and instead of tossing it into the garbage, she brought it outside and let the wind take it away.

She has to empty the pockets furtively, before doing laundry, when Fern is busy doing something else, or she'll get into trouble. This past spring, Fern caught Ruth pulling a blue shard of bird's egg out of her coat pocket and asked, "What are you going to do with that?" The shell had a bit of dried yolk and a wisp of feather stuck to it, but Ruth said, "Nothing," and put it back.

Stef makes a face at Ruth's cereal. "Are you actually going to eat that? It looks like psoriasis."

81

Are you actually going to eat that?

She'd said the same thing long ago in their high-school cafeteria, when Ruth pulled a tiny pink hoof out of her lunch bag. She dropped it on the table immediately, staring at the dainty, thumb-sized body part. The pale, sticky-looking skin. But there was no blood. *Where did all the blood go?*

"Oink, oink," Stef said, and laughed, because they'd dissected fetal pigs that day and Ruth had thrown up, and now she had no appetite for the sandwich and juice box and apple her mother had packed for her, even though, Stef always pointed out, she was old enough to pack lunch for herself.

"Why did you do that?" Ruth asked her in a shaking voice.

Stef's smile disappeared. "I don't know."

Ruth pushes her cereal bowl away and scowls at her wavering reflection in the kitchen table's glossy surface.

She reaches for the newspaper and opens it to an article about a woman who tried and tried to have a baby but could never get pregnant, so eventually she and her husband adopted a little girl from another country. And for a while, they were very happy. Then one day the mother woke up, and while her husband was still sleeping, she bundled their daughter into the car, drove to a forest on the edge of town and left her there.

Ruth folds the newspaper back up.

"Worrying is for suckers." Sammy chomps on a piece of toast and points the crust at Ruth. "Like Marvin says, life is too short."

"You'll worry less when Fern goes to school," says Stef. "You'll have to."

"Maybe," says Ruth.

"Did you bring toilet paper?" Sammy asks her abruptly.

Ruth blinks at him. "What?"

82

"Jesus." He honks a sharp breath out of his nose. "She didn't bring toilet paper."

"Sorry," says Ruth. "Was I supposed to?"

"Sorry won't cut it when I'm mid-shit and staring at an empty roll." He holds up a thick finger. "The rules are: cottage guests have to A) do all the dishes, and B) supply all the toilet paper. Or else they don't get invited back."

"Lay off, Sammy," says Stef. "I didn't tell her, okay?"

"But she should just know. Shouldn't she? When someone does something nice for you, you need to demonstrate your sincere appreciation. Am I right?"

"I appreciate it," Ruth says quickly. "Thank you for having us."

Sammy grabs Stef's arm and pulls her in for a sloppy kiss, exaggerating the smooching sounds until she laughs and pushes him away.

"Don't mention it," she says, but when she catches Ruth's eye, she's not smiling anymore. "So." Stef pulls the knife out of the strawberry-jam jar. "What do you think of our mysterious neighbour, anyway?"

Ruth presses gently on the handle of her spoon, wondering what she'll dredge up. "He's nice, I guess."

"I feel sorry for the guy," says Sammy. "He's got that wife."

"Don't be a jerk!" Stef points the knife at him. "She's the one you should feel sorry for. The woman loves kids but they don't have any. How sad is that?"

Sammy shrugs. "That's why we let her babysit."

Stef laughs at that and licks the knife clean. "But he's cute, right?" she says to Ruth.

"Please," says Sammy, "not while I'm eating."

"I don't know," says Ruth. "I'm tired." She closes her eyes briefly and sees an open doorway. The room beyond is mostly dark, with hardly any light. A tall shape towers inside, but she's smaller so everything is bigger. And Stef's hands are on her back, pushing.

"Marvin might be an only child too, for all I know." Stef wipes a sticky smear of red off the side of her mouth. "I have no idea. He's pretty tight-lipped about family stuff."

"Mama!"

Ruth tries to react more slowly this time. Trying to be a cool, laid-back parent. She turns toward the deck, ready to say, "Monsieur Foomay's in the backpack, remember?"

But Fern isn't there.

She shoves her chair back, nearly toppling Stef. "Where is she? I don't see her." She runs to the screen door and looks out.

The twins are gone. Fern is lying on her back alone on the deck, hog-tied with pink skipping rope.

Ruth rushes out and kneels down, wrestling with the rubbery knots.

Fern is smiling. "We're playing kidnapper."

A FEW HOURS later, Ruth is starting to burn.

She's at the little beach with Sammy and the three girls, and Stef is up in the cottage making lunch.

"Fee, fi, fo, fum. I smell little girls, YUM!"

An ear-splitting screech from Fern and Amelia and Isabelle and they're off, racing across the beach to get away from Sammy, who chases them with his arms raised over his head, hands curled into claws: "The monster is going to *get you!*"

"Ahhhhh!"

The three girls fly toward her and Ruth reaches for Fern, but they keep going, kicking up sand with frantic feet, huge grins stretched wide enough to eat their terrified faces whole.

They love this game so much.

She rubs more sunscreen onto the back of her neck and calls, "Not so close to the shore, please!"

Sammy calls back over his shoulder, "I understand that it's physically possible to drown in an inch of water, but I think they'll be okay."

Ruth sits back and watches them run.

When she and Stef were kids, they loved that game too. Because back then it was fun to be scared. In the daytime, whenever bird shadows darted past Ruth's bedroom window, the two of them would scream, "Bats!" And at night they would huddle together on Ruth's bed and tell each other stories about all the imaginary bad men who wanted to get them. And when they were a little older, they went looking for real ones.

There's a splash from the lake, and Ruth looks over in time to see a gull flapping away with a fish. The silvery-white belly flashes as it wriggles and then the bird flies away and they're gone.

Ruth pulls her phone out of her beach bag and dials into voicemail and lies still while she listens to her mother's sad voice. "I'm glad you're at Stef's new cottage now," her mom says. "It's a good time to be at a cottage." That's all, and then she hangs up.

Ruth thinks about calling her back. She holds the phone in one hand, feeling its weight. The shiny metal is warm in the sun. She slips it back into her bag.

"Hey!" Stef shouts from the staircase, brandishing a picnic basket. "I made sandwiches for the girls. Is your bizarrely healthy child allowed to eat PB&J on Wonder Bread?"

"Not usually," says Ruth. "But what the hell."

Stef grins as she jumps down the last few steps. "That's my girl."

"Yep." Ruth lies back and surrenders herself to the sun. "That's me."

She used to have other friends, she reminds herself, and the memory is comforting. The people she met at university were interesting and kind and easy to talk to, and they thought the same about her. Then she graduated and worked in an office for a while, and she made friends there too.

But Stef didn't get along with any of them. They were too boring, too snobby, too self-absorbed. Never good enough. Which shouldn't have been such a problem. Ruth didn't bring Stef everywhere she went. She had her own life—has her own life. Of course she does. It's just that they have this history. And so do Stef and James. They're all tied up together, too tight to breathe. Stef is like family. That has to count for something. So gradually those other friends dropped away.

Ruth's parents always said that Stef has a big personality, and this is true. Big personalities are sometimes difficult to get along with. They only shine their light on certain people, and Ruth is lucky to be one of them.

Except sometimes she imagines that James is gone and Fern is gone and Stef is the only one left. And of course they're good friends, so that should at least be something. But for some reason, when she really thinks about it, it's not.

Now Ruth can see, as Stef strolls toward her, that the picnic basket is stuffed with junk food, bristling with brightly coloured plastic bags and boxes and tubes.

She sighs and gets to her feet, knees and hips screaming briefly in protest. "I think I'm going to take a little dip."

"Knock yourself out. I'll feed the troops." Stef gives her a once-over. "Cute suit. I like the ruffle."

"Thanks." Ruth is wearing a one-piece and Stef is wearing a bikini, like they always do. "There's some cut-up melon in my beach bag, if you want to give them that too."

"We'll see if they leave any room." Stef winks at her, then hollers, "Kids! Lunchtime!"

The children and Sammy sprint over and descend upon the snacks, tearing open wrappers and spearing juice boxes.

A little treat won't hurt her, Ruth chides herself, and wades backward into the sparkling water until it rises to her shoulders.

She keeps her eyes on Fern, whose face is already smeared with chocolate. Then she inches back until she can't touch the bottom anymore. She feels herself going under and closes her mouth right before the lake rushes in.

She likes it when so much of her is hidden away like this, and she's just a head bobbing on the surface.

At the cottage her parents rented, she liked to sit at the end of the dock and dangle her legs over the edge, submerging one foot at a time. When just her feet were in the water like that, it almost looked as if someone had sawed them off and tossed them into the lake and there they were, floating.

Down below, the blood is barely a trickle now, a few drops staining the pantyliner she'd stuck into her bathing suit earlier. There's nothing else left.

She starts treading water and remembers when she was once hugely pregnant, right near the end, and she and James had gone to a beach in the city to enjoy one of their last days of being just the two of them.

She'd had trouble focusing on him, though, the whole time. She was too busy trying to convince herself that nothing bad was going to happen, but she didn't believe that was true.

Her worry would carry her away for a while, and James would ask, "Where did you go?"

She'd shake her head and tell him, "Just thinking," and try to smile.

87

"Well, don't think too much, okay? There's probably some bad stuff about me in there so the less thinking you do, the more perfect I'll seem."

She'd smiled and then struggled to her feet, almost losing her balance on the rocks, and he caught her before she fell.

"Just relax," he told her. "I'll get whatever you need."

"I think what I need is to be alone in the water for a bit."

There was a flash of hurt in his eyes before he nodded. "Sure."

"I'm lighter there," she added. A feeble joke to take the sting of abandonment away, and she hated herself for not being kinder, happier, more in-the-moment with her wonderful husband who only wanted to take care of her and their unborn child.

"Well, don't drift out to sea on me, now." He grinned. "Even though it's the lake."

She smiled back. "I love you."

"I love you too. I'll be right here."

She picked her way along the pebbly sand, anxious about slicing her feet on one of the sharper stones but determined to get where she was going by herself.

Her body wasn't her own anymore—the baby had taken over the controls. She wobbled everywhere she went, but that beach had thrown her absurd lack of balance into stark relief. She was in danger of tipping over and hurting them both.

But once she was immersed in the cool water, she was safe. Her feet anchored on the smoother sand, her belly no longer so heavy.

She caressed that swollen part of her, dancing her fingers over the tightly stretched skin, and started humming to herself. She liked to change up the words of her favourite songs so they were all about the baby. A silly little exercise to strengthen her imagined connection with the stranger living inside her body.

Stef had already started giving her advice—*do this, don't do that*—because she'd done this all before and she knew everything.

When Ruth visited her in the hospital right after the twins were born, her friend had been triumphantly topless, a baby on each breast. Sammy was standing next to her, spoon-feeding her soup as she nursed. "Look at me!" Stef had crowed. "I'm acing this!"

She told Ruth, "When you start breastfeeding, do not wear a bra or even a shirt for the first two weeks at least. Just let the gals swing free, and let your baby go at you whenever she wants. You'll be exhausted and sore and overwhelmed, but trust me on this. She needs to figure you out and you need to figure her out."

She said that for the first few weeks after the twins came home, Sammy would find dried milk droplets all over the house and he'd joke, "It's like a crime scene in here!" He'd point out the trail of gummy, off-white circles that went all the way up the stairs, and then he'd cross his arms like a TV detective. "Let's examine the breastmilk-spray trajectory," he'd say. "What does it tell us about the terrible events that transpired here?" And sometimes Stef would call him into the bathroom where she'd be leaning over the tub with excess milk streaming from both of her nipples like water from a faucet—it would go that fast—and she'd say, "Check it out! I'm a human fountain!"

Ruth imagined the same thing happening to her, and James would stand in the doorway watching her, his face full of pride and wonder and love and relief. And they'd laugh together about their years of bad luck and how it was actually good luck in the end, because it had been leading up to this all along.

"Mama!"

Fern's voice drags her back, and Ruth takes long, moonwalk leaps from the water to the small, solitary figure waving at her, standing away from the rest of the pack.

"Mama, can I go swimming with you?"

The water gets shallower and gravity increases. By the time she reaches her daughter, she's worn out. She collapses onto the wet sand and pulls Fern onto her lap. "Hmm, I think you should wait a bit. You just ate."

"She's fine," says Stef. "And you just soaked her anyway."

"Yeah!" Fern struggles out of Ruth's embrace and sticks out her bum, displaying the dark patch on her pink-and-purple suit. "You soaked me!"

"All right." Ruth sighs. "Get your floaty on."

"Yay!" Fern pumps her fist in the air. "Floaty!"

"Water wings are for babies," Isabelle jeers.

"It's not water wings, Isabelle," Ruth corrects her in a sing-songy voice. "It's a floaty."

This is what she and James call the stretchy T-shirt attached to a blow-up ring that barely keeps Fern buoyant but allows her more mobility than a life jacket, which Ruth used to insist on, but she'd relented when James explained that part of learning to swim was being able to move one's own limbs in the water.

Fern puts it on and wades into the lake, and then before Ruth realizes what's happening, Fern is swimming away from her—really swimming, moving her arms and legs in a respectable doggy paddle, and the sudden gust of fierce pride somehow overrides Ruth's protective instinct for a few shining seconds, and in that time she catches herself actually enjoying the sight of her child enjoying herself, and it's wondrous.

"Fernie!" Ruth laughs. "You're a fish!"

Look at her, so brave and strong, gaining confidence every minute.

She's so happy! Look at her, swimming all on her own. With just a cheap vinyl flotation device between her and a watery grave.

"Okay," she calls, "turn around and come back to me, please!"

But Fern keeps going.

"Woohoo!" Stef hoots, and Sammy and the girls cheer along with her. "Go, Fern!"

Ruth turns and frowns at them.

"What?" says Stef. "She's doing great!"

And Ruth surges forward, propelling herself toward her daughter, who is way too far out now.

Ruth's feet scrabble against the sand until the water is at her chin, and she kicks her legs hard. With every stroke, she stretches out her fingers for a body part to grab, but the back of Fern's head keeps bobbing along out of reach.

"Fern! Stop!"

And then she does stop. She swivels around, and her beautiful features are all crumpled up, her eyes narrowed and nose crinkled into a snout and lips pulled tight in a snarl. She opens her mouth and howls, savage and furious, "I want to do it MYSELF!"

Ruth falls backward from the words, and then Fern swallows a mouthful of lake and her anger is replaced by fear, the switch of expressions so instantaneous that Ruth starts to doubt she ever saw the first one.

Her daughter bleats out a panicked, "Mama!" and sputters and flails her arms and sinks sideways, and Ruth sees that the ring around her waist wasn't inflated properly, and she should have checked that, *Why the hell didn't she check that?*

She closes the last of the distance between them and clamps an arm around Fern's middle, hugging her tight, but the

91

thrashing limbs are impossible to contain and Ruth can't touch the bottom and she starts to go under herself, taking a deep breath but that's not going to help, she needs something else to keep them both afloat, but there's nothing.

She tries to orient them toward the shore, shoving sideways with one shoulder, tilting her head back and gulping more air but now she's gulping water too, and she chokes and wheezes, desperate to breathe and she can't tell if Fern is breathing either. She's not saying anything, not making any sounds. There's still strength left in her little arms and legs, Ruth can feel that, but she's moving more slowly now.

Ruth tries to call for help but there's no power in the word. The rasping whisper slips out of her mouth and dies on her lips, and she wonders if their friends even know they're in trouble or if they think she and Fern are just splashing around together, having fun. They're not even that far from shore but it's still so far away.

Using all the force she has left, Ruth leans back and pulls her daughter closer so she can boost her up on her chest, giving her all of the air to breathe. The weight of her pushes Ruth down, and she sinks.

But then a miracle happens. A paddle appears in front of her and Ruth latches on, and she and Fern are being pulled to shore and a deep voice is telling them, "You're okay, you're okay, don't worry."

And there is Marvin hovering over them, and then Ruth feels sand under her toes and she lets go but that's a mistake because it's too soon, it's still too deep for Fern, but Marvin is jumping off his board and splashing in with them and lifting Fern up and she's fine, she's clinging to him and coughing and crying, but she's fine.

Ruth heaves a sob and hears herself mumbling, "Thank you thank you thank you."

Marvin places her trembling child into her outstretched arms. "Don't mention it."

SOON AFTER, RUTH and Fern and Stef and Amelia and Isabelle are lined up along the shore, finishing off the last of the junk food and staring out at the lake, where Marvin and Sammy are trying to push each other off their paddleboards and seeing who can stay on the longest.

Fern is swaddled in her towel, the crustaceans' red pincers standing guard.

Ruth holds a small, colourful package over her open palm and the last two FrootSnax fall out. They're like jujubes but apparently healthier, and are shaped like the fruit they're supposed to taste like.

The twins were angry that Stef didn't get the ones shaped like characters from a show Ruth has never heard of, *Rainbow Fashion Fairies* or something similar, and Stef had kicked sand at them until they squealed.

Ruth pops the tiny apple and the tiny orange into her mouth and chews. They're too sweet and they stick to her teeth and she thinks, *I should buy these sometime.*

"Mom," says Isabelle, "we're bored. Can we have our iPads?"

Stef throws her arms wide. "You're at the *beach!*"

Amelia whines, "But we want to play BooBerry Hoedown!"

Isabelle says, "If we go back to the cottage, can we have our iPads there?"

"Forget it! I told you, iPads are off-limits this weekend."

"But *whyyy?*"

93

"Because Fern doesn't have one. So it's not fair to her." Stef pauses. "And Auntie Ruth said so."

The twins turn to Ruth. "But we'll share ours with her! We promise! We'll even let her play *twice*."

"Enough," says Stef. "First of all, you two suck at sharing. Second of all, Fern isn't allowed, so that's the end of the story."

Fern watches their exchange, wide eyes ping-ponging back and forth.

"But why isn't she allowed?" says Isabelle. "That's mean."

Stef looks at Ruth. "You want to take this, or should I?"

Ruth says, "Fern is too young for those games, girls. But thank you for offering to share with her."

Amelia says, "But we know a girl named Yuriah and she's only two and a half and she gets an iPad."

Isabelle adds, "And Yuriah's brother Leaper gets one too and he's only a baby!"

Stef says, "He's not a baby, he's one year old, and their mommy and daddy are morons who named their children Yuriah and Leaper. But if you ever repeat that, I will skin you both alive and use your pelts for picnic blankets, do you understand? Now go play. And take Fern with you."

"But she's just a baby!" says Isabelle.

"She's not a baby," says Stef. "Leaper is a baby. Fern is three."

"Three and a half," says Fern.

"You're almost four, actually," Ruth tells her. "Your birthday's coming up soon."

"My birthday!" Fern lets out a whoop and punches the air.

"Oh yeah." Stef nods. "What's the date again?"

Ruth starts to answer her, but her friend cuts her off and winks at Fern. "Just kidding. I could never forget your birthday! I was there, remember?"

Fern screws up her face in concentration and Stef laughs. "It's okay. You didn't have enough brain cells back then to process sensory details. Your mommy remembers, though."

Ruth's cheeks are too hot and she covers them with her hands. "Of course I do." She remembers the bright room and the smiling doctor and nurses and medical students, and Fern's beautiful wail. She remembers crying with James and the surge of gratitude that rose and then faltered when Stef cracked a joke, making everyone laugh. *Too hot.* She presses her palms against her burning skin, but there's no relief.

"Knock, knock, Auntie Stef," says Fern.

Stef grins at her. "Who's there?"

"Ice."

"Ice who?"

"Ice to meet you!"

Stef applauds. "Ha!"

Ruth says, "I think that one's supposed to be, 'What did the snowman say to the fridge?'"

"Don't correct her," says Stef. "She's perfect."

Out in the water, Marvin and Sammy are charging at each other in slow motion, using their oars like lances.

"What do you want for your birthday, Fern?" Stef asks.

Fern's eyes go glassy. "Toys."

"Nothing electronic, please," Ruth adds.

"Oh, come on," says Stef. "She's turning four!"

Ruth shrugs. "Exactly my point."

Stef leans closer to Fern and whispers loudly, "Maybe Auntie Stef will do a magic trick at your party and make a video game appear. Would you like that?"

"Ooh," says Fern. "I love magic."

A cloud of insects levitates nearby. Tiny blackflies. The mass of them expands and contracts, almost like they're breathing together.

There was a magician at Stef's seventh birthday party. He had a moustache and a tall, black hat, and when Ruth asked him if he had a bunny in there, he said, "Wouldn't you like to know?"

She knotted her fingers together and gazed up at him. "Yes, I would."

He reached down and his eyes were very blue and they made her feel cold as his fingers fluttered behind her ear. And then he was holding up a shiny, gold coin that he'd pulled out of her somehow, from way deep inside, and then Stef was beside her and she grabbed the coin and put it in the pocket of her red corduroy pants and told Ruth, "It's *my* birthday."

And Ruth had to agree.

The magician stood in the centre of Ruth's parents' family room and performed his tricks to a chorus of giggles and oohs and ahhs.

Stef had invited four other girls from their class and none of them were friends with Ruth. They wouldn't even talk to her.

After the magician left, it was time for cake. Ruth sat at her dining-room table, which her mother had decorated with pink streamers, and ate silently while Stef and her guests chattered away. Then one of the girls, whose name was Yolanda, started laughing because Ruth had chocolate icing on her nose.

"It looks like poo!" she shrieked, and Stef reached out and shoved her, almost casually, and Yolanda toppled off her chair and started to cry.

"Don't be mean to my friend," Stef told her, and went back to eating her cake, which was the golden kind with fudge icing, which Ruth's mom had baked for Stef because it was her favourite.

At the end of the party when the guests' parents arrived, Ruth's dad handed the girls their loot bags and they all said thank you, except for Yolanda. They left one by one, the screen door banging shut behind them each time, and then Ruth and Stef were alone again.

"Did you have fun?" Ruth asked her, but Stef just looked out at the empty street.

It was getting dark by the time Stef's mom and dad pulled into the driveway.

Stef and Ruth were still sitting by the screen door and a cool breeze was blowing in while they ate the candy from their loot bags, which had laughing clown faces all over the crinkly paper.

Stef's father stayed behind the wheel and her mother got out of the car. She started walking toward the house and Stef jumped up, grinning.

From somewhere behind them, Ruth's mom said to Ruth's dad in the low voice she always thought was too low for the kids to hear, but it never was, "So nice of them to take time out of their busy schedules."

Ruth's eyes widened, and Stef stopped smiling. She crumpled her loot bag into a hard ball with sharp edges and threw it at Ruth's face. She flung open the screen door and ran down the steps shouting, "I don't even want it anyway!"

Ruth was crying, and her dad knelt down and held onto her as Stef raced toward her mother, who took her hand and ushered her into the back seat, then waved stiffly and climbed back into the front. The car backed up slowly and drove off.

"It's okay, honey," Ruth's dad told her, wiping her tears away. "She'll say sorry later."

Amelia whispers something in her sister's ear, and Isabelle giggles. Then both girls grab Fern's hands and yank her up. "Come with us!"

"Okay," Fern says, and allows herself to be pulled away as Marvin and Sammy amble back over.

Ruth watches the girls go, shielding her eyes against the sun. She wipes her brow and wonders if she might have heatstroke. She's very thirsty. She should get up and look in the cooler for a water bottle.

Sammy shambles stiffly toward Stef with his eyes bugging out and arms thrust forward. "Towel!" he moans. "Give me towel!"

"Get it yourself." She flicks a hand at him. "They're in the beach bag."

He leans over her, reaching, and Stef shrieks, "You're dripping all over me!"

Marvin stops next to Ruth's lounge chair and peers down at her. His surf shorts have sharks on them today, and his feet and ankles are caked with sand. Mud-monster feet. "You look flushed," he says. "I'll get you some water."

She smiles up at him. "Thank you."

"See how easy that was?" Stef mutters.

Sammy gives her a quick look. "What were you ladies talking about?"

She shrugs. "Nothing of consequence."

"Okay." He yanks two towels out of the beach bag and tosses one at Marvin, who's crouching next to the cooler. The red fabric settles over his broad shoulders but falls off when he stands up.

Marvin cracks open a water bottle and hands it to Ruth, and she guzzles it gratefully.

"Hey, hero," Stef drawls, "can I get one of those too?"

"Sorry," says Marvin. "They're all gone."

"Oh." She summons a look of supreme disinterest and makes a show of shaking sand off her towel. "Whatever."

Marvin sits down beside Ruth, and all at once, she's acutely aware of his proximity to her and his distance from Stef. And when she sees Stef noticing this too, a current runs through her. It straightens her back and makes her skin hum, and calls her attention to the soft weight of her hair on her neck. She reaches up and plays with a few strands, twirling them around her fingers.

"We were talking about kids and computers," Ruth tells Sammy, ignoring the brief pang of guilt telling her she should offer some water to Stef. *She'd probably make a joke that it's all backwash, anyway.* She tips the bottle and feels the last few cool drops slide all the way down her throat. "Stef said you guys know some parents who let their one-year-old use an iPad and I thought that was a bit young. Fern doesn't play too many video games yet."

"Do you live under a rock or something?" Sammy asks her. "Did you come to us from the past?"

"I think Ruth's got the right idea," says Marvin. "It's better for kids to be out in nature and experiencing the real world, and socializing with actual people and drawing on actual paper and using their imaginations to make up their own games." He pauses when he sees the other adults staring at him. "I mean, that's what we did when we were little, right? And I keep reading that too much screen time is bad for them, so."

"It is!" says Ruth.

"Aww, look at you two technophobes bonding," says Stef. "So sweet."

Down the beach, the twins point to something by their feet and Fern leans over to look. Then Isabelle pushes her, and Fern falls face-first onto the sand.

Ruth starts to stand up. But Fern doesn't cry, so she sits back down.

The twins are pushing each other over now and all three girls are laughing.

"James calls you his little dinosaur," says Stef. "Did you know that?"

"No." Ruth frowns. "I didn't."

She hadn't grown up on video games like Stef had. Ruth's parents preferred old-fashioned board and card games like Monopoly and Clue and Uno. They let Ruth watch TV, and when she was older, they gave her and Stef handfuls of quarters for Pac-Man and Donkey Kong at the local arcade. But they never saw the point of home computers, while Stef's mom and dad filled their house with all the latest gadgets and didn't care how many hours Stef spent playing alone on her Intellivision or Atari or Commodore 64.

"Did you at least let your daughter watch a movie on the way up here?" Stef asks.

"Fern doesn't need movies in the car. She looked out the window and we played I Spy."

Sammy looks up from scrounging in the picnic basket. "It's a four-hour drive!"

Ruth shrugs. "She had a nap."

"Good for you," says Marvin.

She holds tight to her smug smile, remembering Fern's endless, whining demands from the back seat as the trees and farms and fields blurred by. Her own guilty, fervent wishes for her wonderful daughter to just shut up and fall asleep, and the giddy, overwhelming relief when she finally did.

"Eventually they stop napping, you know," says Stef. "You can't hide from the future forever."

Ruth licks her dry lips. "I'm not hiding." When she crushes the empty water bottle, the crackling of the plastic makes her wince.

"And need I remind you that this terrible, soul-killing technology puts food on both of our tables, and that without it, our children would starve?"

Marvin is watching them intently now, and Sammy is smirking over the handful of broken Doritos he's scavenged.

It's always been this way and it always will be. Stef is the joker and Ruth is the joke.

Stef and James will guffaw over their hilarious anecdotes about people Ruth doesn't know, and Sammy doesn't know half of them either but he'll always laugh anyway. But Ruth will just sit there, trying to remember how it felt to be like them.

"Look at her," Stef will say with an indulgent smile. "Our clueless Ruthie. Isn't she adorable?"

"Her husband and I work together," Stef tells Marvin, stealing nacho crumbs from Sammy's hand. "James is my underling, actually. He's a game designer, and I tell him what games to design."

Their neighbour glances at Ruth. "Interesting."

"It's funny," says Stef. "We both got jobs at the same company after university because it looked like fun. Donut Mondays and Beer Fridays and vintage arcade machines in the break room. But then I shot up the ranks—"

Sammy waggles his eyebrows. "And we all know how *that* happened."

Stef snorts. "It wasn't for my hard work, anyway. It's easy there." She pauses. "It's weird, though—they seem to appreciate me."

"*I* appreciate you," says Sammy, leering.

She ignores him. "So now I'm the big boss earning the big bucks." She crosses her arms and leans back. "And I like it."

"Good for you," says Marvin.

Sammy reaches over and wipes nacho-cheese dust onto his wife's leg. "Ahem. I also put food on the table, hello!"

She swats him away, grinning. "That's right. You pay for the appetizers."

Ruth is about to say, *I used to make money too*, but she doesn't bother.

Her office job was never anything special, and she didn't mind giving it up when she was trying to have Fern. The doctor said maybe taking a leave of absence would reduce her stress, and then James told her she could go ahead and quit if she wanted to because he was making enough by then, so she did. She didn't miss the work and she didn't feel bad about that because she was doing enough already. But sometimes she misses some of the people. She misses their gentle, open faces and the conversations she'd have with them and the jokes they would tell each other, even if they weren't the funniest jokes in the world. Even if the conversations weren't the best ones she'd ever had. They still meant something, and that mattered.

The water laps against the shore, and the kids pick up handfuls of wet sand and carry it farther up the beach where the sand is dry. They let the dark globs drop, bit by bit, onto one spot, then stand around frowning at it.

"Daddy!" yells Isabelle. "Our sandcastle isn't working!"

"You have to use a bucket!" Sammy yells back.

"Help us!"

"You put sand in the bucket and pat it with your hand and then turn the bucket upside-down. Does that sound hard?"

Isabelle puts her hands on her hips and so does Amelia, and both girls glower at him. "We don't want to do it that way!"

Fern sits down with crossed legs and pokes at the mess they've made.

"They're trying to make a drip castle, duh," Stef tells Sammy. "You don't need a bucket for a drip castle."

"What the hell is a drip castle? That's not a real thing."

"It's British. Some British guy at the office told us about it, anyway. We're developing an app where you can make them with magical sparkly sand in all different colours, it's really cool. But I think I can figure it out IRL." She throws a pointed look at Ruth and Marvin. "That means 'in real life,' for the Luddites in the crowd."

Ruth raises her hand and gives it an overeager wave. "I knew that!"

"I didn't," says Marvin.

Ruth smiles at him, and Stef and Sammy walk over to Fern and the twins and start barking instructions.

Ruth and Marvin are silent for a while, watching them, and then Marvin says, "I like how calm you are."

"Me?" Ruth blinks at him. "I'm not calm."

"You are, though. It's amazing." He lowers his voice. "Especially after everything you've been through."

Ruth's mouth opens and closes but no sound comes out. Her pulse quickens as she waits for what he'll say next, but he's quiet again.

They're sitting too close. His bare skin next to her bare skin. She wishes she'd brought her cover-up down here, but it's still folded neatly in her suitcase, not doing anyone any good.

She takes a breath and manages to ask him, "What do you mean?"

103

He doesn't answer right away, and her heart hammers so loudly she's sure he can hear it.

Marvin picks up a small piece of driftwood and turns it around in his hands, then puts it down gently. "Stef told me you had to try for a long time before you had Fern," he says. "That must've been very difficult."

Ruth exhales, picturing her friend radiant and full of knowing. Doling out other people's business in bits and pieces.

"Thank you." She flails around for something nice to say in return. But maybe he never wanted kids to begin with, so a sorry would fall flat. He doesn't need her pity if he's living the life he wanted all along. He doesn't need it either way.

So she just offers another faint smile, and that seems to be enough because he smiles back. His hair is much darker than James's. And his nose is bigger, but in a nice way. And he has a nice, square jaw with nice stubble all over it. She always likes how stubble looks, but it's so scratchy. Sometimes James will rub her face raw when they kiss, and she'll have marks the next day.

She feels herself blushing and looks away, and so does Marvin. They both swivel their heads to watch the drip castle taking shape and growing taller.

The twins and Fern take turns letting the wet sand fall from their fingers, forming peaks and turrets and an uneven wall surrounding them. Their expressions alternate between fierce glee and stern, single-minded absorption.

Sammy stands back and observes, nodding. "Okay, this is pretty cool. But I still think it would be easier with a bucket."

"That's not the *point*, though," says Stef.

He glances at her. "Is the British guy good-looking?"

She shrugs. "Yeah, I guess."

"I'll kill him."

"Please don't. He's a valuable member of our team."

"Is he the one who implants the chips in the kids' brains?" Ruth deadpans.

Marvin and Sammy chortle at that, and Stef suddenly wheels around and staggers back over, jerking her head to the left and right with her eyes full of terror, and jabs a finger at Ruth. "Oh my God, it's *you*! The Anachronistic One who has appeared to herald the BooBerry Apocalypse, which basically looks like a bunch of parents who are overworked and underpaid and exhausted and just need a few minutes to themselves once in a while, so they let their kids manipulate some digital strawberries around a haunted digital field so the poor, undead digital farmer can get a break once in a while too!"

"Okay, okay." Ruth holds up her hands, laughing. "You win."

Marvin plucks an empty FrootSnax pouch off the ground and crumples it into a ball. "I guess I'm lucky I don't have to worry about that stuff."

Before anyone can reply, Fern comes running back over, and Marvin grins at her.

"Mama! Let's dig!"

"Sounds good to me." Ruth finds two shovels in the pile of sand toys. She hands one to Fern and they get to work.

"Can I help?" Marvin asks.

"No." Fern shakes her head solemnly. "You're going to go in the hole we make."

"Am I, now?" His smile broadens.

"You're outnumbered, pal. Get used to it." Sammy opens the cooler and hands him a beer.

Marvin opens it and takes a big drink. "You guys are the best."

"Give me one of those," says Stef. "And Ruth needs one too."

Sammy doles out more silver cans, which glint and flash in the afternoon light.

Ruth pries up the tab on hers and takes a sip. The beer is delicious and cold, and the sun is so hot.

Every summer now reminds her of the last time she was pregnant. When she got all the way to the end. And it was funny, but not really, how an entire season that was previously vivid with so many associations could be overshadowed by a single memory. But it's a big one. It takes up a lot of room.

She wasn't drinking beer then. She couldn't even drink lemonade because it gave her acid reflux. And she was sweaty all the time, but she didn't mind. She didn't mind any of it.

Afterward, though, there was a lot of pain. The birth had torn her open, and it took a very long time to recover. She had to shuffle when she walked, inch by inch.

The twins run over and kneel next to Fern and start pawing at the sand with her.

Stef tosses a couple of shovels at her daughters. "You'll never bury Uncle Marvin at that rate. Step it up!"

The girls' trench gets deeper but not longer. It's large enough now for one of them to lie in, but not nearly large enough for an adult.

"The size is wrong," says Marvin. "It's too small. You have to make it bigger."

The sharpness in his voice makes Ruth look over.

"Whoa, now," Stef says to him. "Bossy, much?"

"Sorry." He looks dazed for a moment, but then he's grinning again. "Guess what? Lesley and I are having a bonfire tonight! That's what I came over to tell you guys. You can't miss it."

"Nice!" says Sammy. "Marvin and Lesley's bonfires are legendary," he tells Ruth. "Everybody goes."

"I shall put on mascara for the occasion," says Stef. "Even though Sammy hates it when I wear eye makeup. He's fine with lipstick. How can you be fine with lipstick and not eye makeup?"

Sammy hoists his can high. "Because when you do your eyes, you look like a whore."

"Whores can be nice sometimes," says Marvin.

Everyone looks at him, and a few seconds later he laughs.

"Sounds like fun," Ruth says.

Marvin takes another drink and raises his can in a toast. "Barry the treasure where no one can find it!"

"Hey!" says Fern. "That's my joke!" Her mouth is set in grim determination as she continues to dig, and the hole gets deeper.

She had the same expression a few nights before, when Ruth came home from grocery shopping and smiled at the hush that greeted her, imagining her husband and daughter snuggled up on the couch with a storybook, or sitting side by side on the floor building Lego towers.

It was *really* quiet, though. Even if they were reading or doing something else low-key, she would've heard something.

"Fern?" she called. "James?" She walked down the hall to the family room. There were so many rooms in the new house. "Hellooo! Where's my family?"

Fern was alone on the big wooden rocking chair that Ruth kept meaning to get rid of, but they'd still dragged it with them when they moved. It was a hopeful wedding gift from James's parents and it had always been uncomfortable. When Fern was a baby, Ruth would rock her in it while she guzzled her bottles like she was starving, and Ruth's back would ache for hours afterward.

Fern was wearing James's headphones, which made her small face appear even smaller, and she didn't look up.

"Hi, Fern! Where's Daddy?"

No response. Fern was focused on something in her lap. Ruth moved closer and removed the headphones.

Fern flinched but didn't look up from James's phone. Her gaze was fixed on the screen, her little thumbs hammering away. "Hi, Mama! I'm making the watermelon soldiers shoot the papaya guards with their seed guns! I'm winning, Mama!"

"Good for you, honey." She moved away and went farther down the hall to the kitchen, where James was tending to a bubbling pot of pasta.

He turned and grinned at her, opening his arms wide. "I'm making the three of us a romantic dinner, with candles and everything!"

"Why is she on your phone?"

James kept his voice light. "I just showed her some games. She wanted to see them, so I showed her."

"She wouldn't know about them if you hadn't told her they existed."

"Ruth, come on. You're overreacting."

"What the fuck, James."

"Keep your voice down." He jerked his head back at the family room.

"Well, luckily you've turned her into a zombie, so she has no idea what's going on beyond the watermelon soldiers killing the mango brigade."

"Papaya guards."

"Did you just correct me on the type of *fruit* in your horrible game?"

His shoulders slumped. "I'll take the phone away from her when dinner's ready, it's not a big deal."

Her eyes were stinging. "But it is."

James sighed. "Here we go."

"I specifically said no phones, no laptops, no tablets, no *anything* like that until she's five. Is she five?"

"Ruth, seriously. She's going to go to school and she'll be the only kid who doesn't know how to use a computer."

"No, she'll be the only kid with social skills and an attention span that lasts more than two minutes at a time."

"Why can't you just be happy here?" He spat the question out. "We have everything we want now. Just be happy."

"STOP IT!"

They both froze.

Fern was standing in the doorway, the headphones lifeless at her feet. She was holding Monsieur Foomay with shaking hands.

Ruth stretched out her arms. "Fernie."

Fern levelled the dragon first at Ruth and then at James. "Stop saying mean things right now or we are going to burn you."

"We'll stop." James held up his hands. "We promise."

Fern dropped her toy and sank to the floor, and the two of them rushed to her side, rubbing her back, telling her it's okay, don't worry, Mommy and Daddy love each other, we were just having an argument and grown-ups do that sometimes, but that's silly, isn't it, because you shouldn't fight with the people you love.

But then Fern was wailing and shrieking, flinching away from them. She ran back to the family room and dumped out her biggest toy bin. "Look, I made a mess! Yell at me!"

Ruth and James stood together at the edge of the spilled Lego and puzzle pieces and sparkly dress-up fairy wings and a plastic wand studded with plastic jewels and scattered plastic medical instruments from a doctor kit—a stethoscope, a blood-pressure cuff, a needle. And all the stuffed animals that Ruth kept giving Fern in the hopes that one of them would replace Monsieur Foomay in her affections—bears and frogs and elephants and lambs—but none of them ever did.

FIVE

THE WIFE LIES ON HER SIDE OF THE BED THAT SHE SHARES with her husband. He already left for work and she is alone, but there's a baby growing inside her again and this time she's sure it will keep growing. She doesn't want to believe that yet, though—doesn't want to hope even a little bit. Because they have been trying and trying and it never works. It always ends in bleeding.

But hope is there anyway.

Yesterday she visited their fertility doctor again, who ordered the test that the wife is so familiar with now. The one that checks the level of pregnancy hormone in her blood, at the very beginning. If the number is high, that's good. If the number is low, that's not good.

Before the doctor sent her on her way, she said to the wife in her kind, compassionate voice, "You need to keep in mind that there are literally a million tiny things that have to go right for conception to succeed. Babies are, quite literally, miracles."

Then the nice nurse who works literally next door to the doctor's office pricked the wife with a needle with that gentle manner she has. She's always so careful not to make it hurt too much. The wife appreciates that.

She used to be very squeamish and would have to lie down or she would pass out, but over the years, it got so she could sit up and be totally fine and she started joking with the nurse that she was a pro now, and the nurse would nod and smile and turn away.

This morning, after the husband left for the tall, shiny office tower where he brings entire new worlds to life, the doctor called with the results. And she told the wife they were good. She has always called and said the results were not good, but this time she said they were good.

112

Now the wife has the same feeling she had so many years ago, before things went wrong and before she even knew about the doctor's test, when she thought it would be easy. When she couldn't wait to show her husband the plus sign that had formed in the tiny window of the plastic purple wand she'd wrapped up in toilet paper and hidden away until he came home. And when he gave her a gift that was a pun about everything they had to look forward to.

The wife curls into a C shape and looks out the window. It's bright and sunny outside and she should call her husband with the news, but she doesn't want to yet. This time she'll wait, keep the secret to herself for a while. Let him guess it on his own when she can't hide it anymore. When she's bursting with the news.

She grins at her own little joke, and because she can't wait to see the look on her best friend's face.

She grins because she told her husband she wanted one more try and at first he didn't think that was a good idea.

He said, "What if something worse happens?"

She said, "It won't." Even though she's afraid of that too.

Because she has heard stories. Friends of friends who gave

birth to stillborn babies at six, seven, eight months along. The mothers had to be induced so they could go into labour and deliver the child they knew was dead, had already died inside them but didn't want to leave. Those babies wanted to stay but they couldn't, so they had to be pushed and pulled out. And it wasn't right for them to stay, even though their mothers would have let them, would have gladly agreed to be a home to those dead babies until they died themselves.

But it's going to be all right. She'll be very, very careful.

And when the wife gives birth to their happy, healthy baby, she will not say to her husband, "See? I told you!" She will be a living, breathing I-told-you-so. And he will love her for it.

For now, though, for a while, she rests here with her hands on her belly, which has never been flat, and has never been round either, and tries not to worry.

On the other side of the window, there are so many people doing all the things that people do. Having breakfast, taking showers, arriving at the office, checking their email, shopping for groceries, reading parenting magazines in doctors' offices because that's the only reading material available.

But on this side, it's just the two of them, and she whispers, "Please." She closes her eyes. "Please stay."

SIX

A FEW HOURS LATER, FERN IS STILL PLAYING IN THE sand, Isabelle and Amelia are wading in the lake, Sammy is off somewhere paddleboarding, Stef is sunning herself, and Marvin is back at his own cottage doing "bonfire prep," which he explained basically meant stockpiling sticks and opening a few bags of chips and making sure there was enough hand sanitizer by the outhouse. And also drinking heavily, ha ha.

Ruth is drinking too, because it's easier that way.

It occurs to her that if she drank like this at home, she'd have a problem. But they're on Cottage Time so what the hell.

They're all still in their swimsuits and they've stopped applying sunscreen. Skin is starting to turn pink.

Stef's fingers dance across her C-section scar. She's always touching it, even when she's dressed. She'll reach down and run her thumb over the place between her hips where that little line glows. Sometimes she'll even sneak a furtive hand inside her waistband, so quickly it might seem to someone else that she was scratching an itch. But Ruth knows what she's really doing.

"It's something I'm good at," Stef likes to say. "I'm a master baby-maker."

Even after she'd only done it once, she was the expert.

Ruth crumples her empty beer can and drops it onto the sand, and Stef immediately reaches into the cooler between them and hands her a full one.

She considers saying no, but it's easier to say nothing and take the can. She won't have it right away. She'll have it later.

She lies back on her lounge chair and closes her eyes, and the blue sky fills with clouds that darken to an angry, boiling green. They clot into a fierce mass and the wind screams and twists it into a funnel that whips the water into giant waves. The cyclone picks up speed, seething with jagged shells and stones and gasping fish. It races toward the shore, where Ruth and James and Fern are building a sandcastle together. And they don't even notice the tornado until it's right on top of them, because they are all so happy and they love each other so much.

Stef's voice drifts toward her. "I was worried about Marvin too, when we first moved in."

Ruth's eyelashes flutter open and she sits up, blinking. The sun is so bright.

"We'd only been here a few days, and then one morning we were all swimming and he came sailing over to say hello."

Out in the water, Isabelle and Amelia start splashing each other. Then they stop.

Fern is making a sand angel on the shore in front of them. She's lying on her back and moving her arms and legs up and down.

"He had his wife's peach pie balanced on his board, and I kept waiting for it to fall into the lake but it never did. He slid right up beside me and handed me the dish—it was still warm—and he said, 'Would one of you fine folks like to join me on a tour of the fiefdom?'"

All of a sudden, Amelia and Isabelle charge out of the lake, flinging water at Fern with their combined full force. She covers her face with her hands and rolls onto her belly, and Ruth is ready to stand up but Stef yells, "Leave her alone, you two!" She shakes her head. "Fucking savages."

The twins run back into the water, and Fern calmly begins gathering stones.

Ruth is still stiff in her chair, and Stef slides her sunglasses down her nose to look at her. "James told me you were concerned about our kids being at the same school."

"What?" Sweat slithers down Ruth's neck. "I didn't—"

"You're overreacting," James had repeated at the end of their last fight, after they'd put Fern to bed and the argument shifted from the evils of electronics to Stef, like it always did. "So they'll be at the same school, big deal. They're her *friends*." He was scraping the remains of their spaghetti dinner into the garbage. Fern had only eaten a few bites of hers. She said she wasn't hungry.

"I wasn't even talking about that," said Ruth. "I never said that."

His back was to her so she couldn't see his face when he muttered, "They're practically her sisters."

"That's my point, though."

The knife James was using squealed against the red-spattered plates. "You always worry about the wrong things."

A scrap of cloud passes over the sun, moving fast although there's scarcely any breeze. It's thin and ragged, but its shadow still makes things dark for a long moment before it's gone.

"I'm just bugging you." Stef nods at the three girls with a smirk. "I'd be concerned too. My kids are jerks. But Fern will be fine. She'll toughen up and grow her shell, like we all do."

Fern starts tossing pebbles into the lake while the twins bob up and down a few metres away, and Ruth relaxes a little. "So what happened with Marvin?"

Stef yawns and stretches and lies back. "Here's this guy we don't know asking us to go paddling off who knows where with him, and I'm thinking, *Nope*, because of course that's the right thing to think in those situations."

"Of course." Ruth nods.

Her friend's hands were on her back, pushing.

They were eleven years old and Ruth didn't want to meet the man in the dark park bathroom, but Stef thought it would be funny. Ruth didn't want him to kiss her, but he did.

"But then Sammy's hauling our new paddleboard into the water and saying, 'Yeah! Sounds great!' And I tell him, 'You can hardly even stand up on that thing, bozo. Plus we don't have any life jackets.' Because the previous owners left us their board and their boat but not their life jackets, jackasses. And he says, 'Marvin's not wearing one!' All pouty like a baby. So I say, 'Whatever,' and Marvin gives me this big, old creepy smile and says, 'Don't you fret, I'll take good care of him.' And Sammy somehow managed to get on and stay upright, and they both sailed away."

The room was dark because it was so bright outside. But the silvery sinks behind the man were shiny in spite of the darkness. She wondered how that could be. He put his big hands on her small shoulders and spun her all the way around and pressed her back against the wall, which was cool against the bare places of her warm skin. Beside her the taps were glinting, like stars.

Then he was pulling her close and bending down so his face was level with hers, and his eyes were big black circles like a cartoon and then his tongue was in her mouth, squirming. Suffocating her so she couldn't scream, and that time was forever but then her friend was there, saving her. Tugging her back toward the open mouth of the room where the sun was blasting in, shouting at him to let Ruth go, "You creepy old man, let her go!" So he did. He slunk back into the shadows, mumbling, "I'm not that old, you know."

And then it was just the two of them again, in the middle of the day in the park where nothing bad could ever happen, and Stef grabbed her hand and they ran to the playground together. They picked swings side by side, like they always did, and swung and swung, back and forth, until they were sick of it.

"Two hours went by," Stef goes on. "Where the hell were they? And I'm telling myself, *Everything's fine. Marvin's a good guy.* Then I think, *But how do you know?* Something bad had definitely happened. Way too much time had passed. So I said to the girls, 'Mommy's going to take the boat out and look for Daddy.' And they got all whiny. 'Whyyyyy?' *Because Marvin might kill him so he can come back and claim us as his own family, idiots.* I didn't say that, obviously. But then I remembered about the life jackets, and I pictured myself falling out of the boat and drowning and then who'd protect the twins, and I know I say I can't stand them most of the time, but every once in a while they do something cute and I'm glad they exist." Stef pauses to crack open a new beer. "A few minutes later, Sammy and Marvin came back and we all got drunk together."

"Wow," says Ruth.

"Yep," says Stef. She takes a breath and the two of them sit there, watching their kids play.

Everything seems fine, so Ruth closes her eyes again. The sun warms her face.

"It helps that he's hot, though, right?" Stef's languid voice slides along the sand between them. "If he was creepy *and* ugly, I wouldn't keep inviting him back."

From out in the lake, Amelia shouts, "Ferrrrn! Look what *we* got!"

Ruth opens her eyes. The twins are holding up Fern's towel, which is now soaking wet.

"Boo-hoo!" Isabelle taunts. "The baby crabs drowned!"

"They're not crabs!" Fern yells. "They're lobsters!" She swings her small arm through the air and Amelia yelps, "Ow!"

The twins back up unsteadily, flailing under the weight of the drenched terry cloth.

Fern's arm flicks again and there's a small splash in front of the girls.

Isabelle hollers, "Mom! She's throwing rocks at us!"

"What?" Ruth leaps out of her chair. "Fern! Stop that!"

"See?" Stef grins. "She's getting tougher already."

THE DAY PASSES and Ruth drinks more. Not so much that she loses the ability to parent effectively, but just enough to smooth out the edges of the late afternoon, and then the early evening. Enough so she doesn't have to think so much about everything.

She knows it's not good to worry. It's not healthy and it doesn't help anyone. She once heard on the radio that worrying actually meant you were directing negative energy at the person you were worrying about, and Ruth doesn't want to do that. She heard it was a better idea to picture that person in a situation with the best possible outcome, and that made a lot of sense to her. It sounded nice. The radio expert was a Tibetan monk, or else somebody quoting a Tibetan monk. Ruth doesn't know anything about Buddhism but the speaker had a very calm voice, which made her want to believe him.

She's alone on the beach now. Stef and Sammy and the twins and Fern are in the cottage, and Marvin is gone but they'll see him later. The same applies to James, actually. Isn't that funny?

She's not the only one who worries, either. James has a particular tone of voice that he only ever uses when he's anxious about Fern.

Recently he was giving her a bath upstairs at the new house and Ruth was downstairs on the living-room couch trying to read a parenting magazine, but the words kept blurring together and she couldn't concentrate on any of the articles, even the ones that looked interesting, and then she heard James call out, "Ruth," in that tone.

She dropped the magazine on the floor and ran up the stairs two at a time, and her heart was pounding so hard and what could be wrong? What terrible thing had happened? And she stopped in the doorway and there were her husband and child, and everything was fine, but James pointed at a tiny mole on Fern's arm and said, "What's that?"

"It's a mole," said Ruth.

"Was it there yesterday?"

"Maybe. I don't know. Sometimes she grows new moles."

"It just looked weird," he said.

"What looks weird?" said Fern.

"Nothing." Ruth smiled at her. "You've got a lot of bubbles in there."

Fern scooped some up with a pink plastic spoon. "We're playing ice-cream store."

James was still staring at the mole.

"Do you want me to finish giving her the bath?" Ruth asked him.

"No, no," he said. "You go back downstairs and relax."

So she left them alone again and returned to her magazine. She opened it up to a bright, glossy spread showing how parents could organize all of their children's toys into "classic" plastic milk crates in different colours, which could be neatly stacked on top of and beside each other to create a "funky retro Rubik's Cube effect."

Then there was a loud bang and some frenzied splashing and she threw down the magazine and ran up the stairs, imagining Fern's head smashing against the porcelain after a slip and fall, her hair matted with blood, James weeping over the tub while the mountain of foam turned pink as Fern sank beneath it, unmoving.

When she reached the doorway, though, Fern was still fine. Everything was fine, but Ruth pretended she had to pee so she could sit on the toilet until bath time was over.

"Okay if the girls watch more TV?" Stef calls from the stairs. Ruth waves a hand at her. "Fine."

"I like you when you're like this." Stef laughs. "You're very pliable."

Ruth glances behind her but sees only trees, so she turns back to gaze at the water again. The lake is very still and she pictures it filling with soap bubbles, frothy and white, rising and expanding to obscure the dock and the boat and the boat's little house and the sky and the sun. Until everything is scrubbed clean and there's nothing left for her to worry about.

There's always something, though. Because anything can go wrong at any time. At any moment, the very worst thing can happen. And she knows this is true.

Her father's heart attack happened two months after the baby was born. He collapsed where he was standing in his backyard and fell face-first onto the grass, and he was still lying there like that when Ruth's mother came home from the grocery store. She saw him through the sliding glass doors in the kitchen when she was unpacking a basket of strawberries, which she dropped and then trampled in her rush to get outside.

A doctor later told her and Ruth that he wouldn't have felt much pain—"just one big blast of it and then he would've been gone."

Ruth's mom nodded mutely when he said that.

She ran back inside to call 911 but didn't call Ruth until after the ambulance had come and carried them away and then he was pronounced dead at the hospital, because she said she didn't want Ruth to worry.

So Ruth didn't feel too guilty about stopping at the mall to buy a black dress on the way to meet her mom in the waiting room, even though she was dimly aware that it was a strange thing to do. Her brain and her body were still so wobbly then. Nothing about her was behaving the way it was supposed to. The birth had been a traumatic one, and she thought she would never heal.

In his small, stuffy office with bright anatomy posters on the beige walls, the doctor interlaced his long fingers and squeezed them together in a slow, steady pulse. "We had a mom and a couple kids in here earlier today with a dad who shot himself in the shower. The youngest girl was the one who found him." He pulled his hands apart and laid them on his desk, pressing them down and flattening them out. "You can at least be grateful that you don't have to deal with something like that."

The door was open and there was so much activity going on in the hallway outside. A cleaner strolled past with a mop. A nurse hurried by with a clipboard. Orderlies in pale-green scrubs wheeled beds with moaning, alive people on them.

"Thank you for telling us that," said Ruth. "It's very considerate of you."

The doctor cocked his head and gave her an uncertain smile, like she'd just shared a joke with him that he didn't quite get.

Her mom looked at her too, because Ruth wasn't normally sarcastic like that.

That was how Stef talked.

And there in the airless little box of an office that the doctor had trapped them in with his stupid platitudes, under a poster of the human body with its skin stripped off so all of the veins and arteries and organs were visible, Ruth felt as if her best friend were stretching inside of her, occupying all of the space that was weak and making it strong.

She had the power to do anything right then. She could've punched the doctor in his face and her knuckles wouldn't even have bruised. She could've slammed her fist into his nose and cheeks and eyes until he was a bloody mess of broken bones and ruined flesh and then just stood up and put an arm around her sobbing mother's shoulders and walked out like nothing had happened.

But he had a framed photo on his desk of a laughing woman with long, curly hair who was holding a laughing, bald baby very tightly, and there was drool on the baby's lips—they were shining with it—so Ruth just stood up and put her arm around her sobbing mother's shoulders and they walked out of the room and left the hospital and went to a fast-food restaurant for dinner but only ate a few of their fries and that was all.

Then they went back to the house and Ruth helped her mom clean the ruined strawberries off the kitchen floor and then they fell asleep together in Ruth's mom's bed, and neither of them woke up for a long, long time.

"Sammy just fired up the barbecue." Stef's voice drifts toward her from somewhere high above the trees. "We should all probably eat something other than chips and Goldfish crackers."

"Hmm?" The word buzzes up Ruth's throat and hangs in front of her. Such an easy thing to say, requiring hardly any effort at all. She didn't even have to open her mouth.

"Drink this, you'll like it," said a tall, freckled boy a long time ago. He'd mixed up the frozen cocktails in his parents' blender with his shorter, uglier friend while Ruth and Stef sat together on his parents' couch in his parents' basement rec room, which had a bar in it, like in a movie for adults.

Ruth had never had a frozen cocktail before. She and Stef were fourteen and they'd met the boys at the mall, where they went because it was air-conditioned and because there were always boys there.

The school year was almost over and summer holidays were starting soon. Outside the boy's parents' house, the late afternoon was sweltering. Inside, under a ceiling fan that turned and turned but barely made a breeze, Stef leaned closer to her and whispered, "I get the cute one."

Ruth nodded as beads of sweat squeezed out all over her. Somehow Stef never got sweaty back then, even on the hottest days.

The couch was actually a loveseat and she and Stef were squashed together on it. She could feel the heat of her friend's bare thigh pressed against hers. They were both wearing shorts and their brand-new matching terry-cloth halter tops. Ruth's was maroon and Stef's was royal blue, and Ruth had been happy enough with the outfit in the change room where she and Stef had posed for each other in the mirror, but then she wished she hadn't changed out of her regular T-shirt.

The blender stopped roaring and Ruth asked the tall boy, quietly, "Where's your mom and dad?"

He said, "Who cares?"

Stef shrieked out a laugh that hurt Ruth's ears.

The loveseat was velour with a flower pattern. Big, fat roses in pink and red and yellow. *Yellow roses are for friendship*, Ruth thought.

"You guys better not mess with us because we're tough," Stef told the boys, making her voice low and serious. "We cut up baby pigs today. Then Ruth puked all over her desk and the janitor had to come and clean it up. It was really gross."

"Don't worry." The tall boy smirked at them from the bar. "We won't cut you up. But don't puke on us, okay?" He winked at Ruth, and she wanted to touch every one of his freckles.

Then his ugly friend, the one Ruth was getting, was handing her a tall, plastic glass fogged with condensation, filled to the brim with orange slush, and she was saying, "Thank you," and giving him her best come-hither smile, which Stef had helped her practise in the change room, and the tall guy was slipping a straw between Stef's glossy lips.

They drank their drinks, and when they were done, they politely commented on how delicious they were, even though Ruth didn't like hers because it was way too sweet. But at least it was cold. Then the boys took the girls' empty cups away and sat down beside them, squashing them even more.

An action movie was playing on the TV, and the handsome hero was running through a field to save his beautiful wife from an evil king. The king had the woman's arms pinned behind her back and his pointy beard was grazing her shoulder.

Stef's guy reached behind him and grabbed a blanket that was resting across the back of the couch. He shook it out neatly and laid it over all of their laps.

The hero sprinted toward the barbed-wire fence between him and his beloved, and the evil king stared him down.

Stef's guy put his hands under the blanket and told everyone else they should do the same.

The king grabbed the struggling woman's hands, guided them onto the wire, and forced them slowly along the length of it. And the woman on TV screamed and screamed.

"Yep." Stef is suddenly on the beach beside her, taking charge. "You definitely need some real food."

Ruth blinks up at her and Isabelle and Amelia and Fern, all of them circled around her lounge chair. Peering at her curiously.

Earlier, before they went up to the cottage to watch TV, Fern and the twins had taken turns burying each other in the sand. They were experts now, after burying Marvin.

Fern reaches out and tickles the bottoms of Ruth's feet, giggling.

"Hey, stop!" Ruth flinches back. "I'm awake."

"You'd better be," Stef tells her. "Because we've got a long night ahead of us." She claps her hands. "Dinnertime, let's go!"

"Hurry up, Mama!" says Fern. "I'm hungry."

"That's why we're having dinner, sweetheart," says Stef. "And also so your mommy doesn't fall on her face."

Fern wrinkles her brow. "Why would she do that?"

"Because she drank too much ALCOHOL!" shouts Isabelle.

Ruth glares at her friend's child, then concentrates on standing up without tipping over.

Stef holds out her hand but Ruth shakes her head. "I'm fine."

"Okay." Stef grins. "If you say so."

"I have to go pee," Ruth had told the ugly boy when he started to climb on top of her. "I have to go really badly."

"Fine," he said. "But you better get back here fast, or else I'll come and get you."

He moved aside and Ruth stood up, and Stef looked up at her from under the cute, freckled boy who was pressing her down and moving his hands around under the blanket. Then she looked away, and Ruth was free.

They all start up the stairs together, two big and three little sets of knees and elbows bending, feet raising and lowering, and then they turn a corner and there is the wasps' nest. Hanging over their heads, beckoning them closer.

Just steer clear of them and they'll steer clear of you.

The nest is moving slightly, and a low, angry hum is coming from the swollen centre of it. It's fascinating, really, this dry, grey husk full of activity. All that life going on inside. Ruth imagines smashing it open like a pinata at a kids' party. How much fun that would be, until it wasn't. They were always filled with such disappointing candy.

"Ruth," says Stef, and she's much farther up the staircase now, herding Fern and Isabelle and Amelia ahead of her. "You need to keep walking or you're going to get stung."

She was out of breath when she got to the top of the basement stairs and she was in the boy's kitchen and *where was the phone?* She scanned the room until she saw the curly cord dangling—her dad liked to call it a piggy tail—and she rushed over and picked up the receiver and dialled her parents' number with a shaking hand.

The humming increases. Any second now, an angry swarm will fill the air around her. Then she'd have to run, but the wasps would be faster. The pain would be everywhere and she'd trip and lose her balance, and for a long, slow-motion moment, she'd be suspended with her arms outstretched, teetering above lake and trees and sky. And then she'd fall.

"Hello?" said her father, and she was crying by then so she couldn't even talk properly.

"Ruthie," he said, "what's wrong?"

"I'm at a boy's house," she managed. "I want to go home."

"Move," says Stef. "Now."

"Tell me the address. I'll be right there."

"I don't know." She glanced at the door to the basement, which she'd left wide open.

"Look around. Is there any mail? Look for an envelope and then read me the address on it."

She scanned the room again and there was a basket on the kitchen table with apples and papers inside. She set the handset on the counter and hurried over and grabbed an envelope from the pile and hurried back. She read the address to her dad and he said, "Go outside and wait for me."

"Okay," she said, and she hung up and ran.

"Mama," says Fern, "what's wrong?"

The little voice finally wakes her up and she moves away, leaving the danger alone so it will leave her alone too. She climbs the stairs until the angry hum subsides and she can smile and tell her daughter, "Nothing's wrong, honey."

She was sitting on the boy's front steps when her dad pulled into the driveway, and then the front door opened behind her and Stef was there.

"You didn't come back," she said.

Ruth blinked in the bright sun, which glinted off her parents' car and made it even shinier. "I was going to."

"Sammy!" Stef hollers. "Slap some extra cheese on Ruth's burger! And get me the can of Raid because I need to do some killing."

The two of them had climbed into the back of the car together and buckled their seat belts without a word.

Ruth's dad stared at them in the rear-view mirror. "Is everybody all right?"

129

Ruth glanced at Stef, who was looking straight ahead, and gave him a tiny nod.

"Good," he said, and reversed out of the driveway and drove down the street, and the house got smaller and smaller until it was gone.

Ruth huffs and puffs up the last few steps and watches Fern and Amelia and Isabelle run into the cottage, giggling and squealing and safe.

Her friend stands at the top with her arms crossed. "I'm more responsible than you today," she says. "Sometimes Auntie Stef's not so bad after all."

From the tree branches overhead, the incessant electric whine of all the hidden cicadas rises in volume, filling the air until there isn't room for any more sounds, and then it stops. Ruth has always wondered what makes them go quiet like that. She saw a dead one once, at the cottage with her parents. Her dad told her it was a tiny alien that had crash-landed on Earth, and she was sad that it was never going home.

"You're going to spray the nest now, right?" says Ruth.

Stef arches an eyebrow. "What do you say?"

The cottage towers above them, blank windows reflecting the sun. Making Ruth squint. "Please?"

"Well, okay then." Stef gives her a brisk nod. "Since you asked so nicely."

BY THE TIME she's changed into shorts and a T-shirt and is sitting at the picnic table on the screened porch with a big glass of water and a giant cheeseburger in front of her, Ruth is feeling better.

The twins are showing Fern something on their iPads, which apparently are no longer off-limits, but why should Ruth care? It's not much different than TV, right? And video games are her husband's job! They can't be all bad. It's fine.

She even laughs at one of Sammy's jokes, something about a porcupine hiding in an outhouse with disastrous consequences, and he grins at her and says, "Glad to see you're finally on Cottage Time."

Ruth nods, and the movement feels bigger than usual.

The lamp that hangs over the picnic table is swaying in the breeze. Inside it, the small, dark shapes of dead and dying bugs clutter the frosted glass.

Stef had aimed the nozzle of the Raid can at the small hole at the bottom of the wasps' nest and counted slowly to ten as she filled it up with poison. "This is the best time of day to do it, actually," she said, "when they're the least active. They're all in there chilling out with the queen. We have to get them all, but especially her. If you let that bitch go free, she'll just keep on pumping 'em out somewhere else."

Ruth had nodded from a few feet away, muscles tensed to start running.

They were both still wearing their bathing suits—she'd suggested they put on more protective clothing first but Stef had said, "You want to do this now, or not?"

When she was done spraying, Stef lifted the nozzle to her lips and blew on it like it was a smoking gun. "That was extremely satisfying," she sighed, her other hand resting on her smooth, tanned belly.

Ruth's skin was so much paler, and her suit was riding up again. She tried to pick it out discreetly, waiting for Stef to catch her and say something sarcastic, but her friend was too busy drumming her fingers on that raised pink line between her hips, a few inches below her belly button.

Ruth wondered if the workers inside the nest had any idea. Maybe one of them was dragging himself over to the queen right at that moment, telling her to hurry up and get the hell out before it was too late. Maybe the queen had just enough strength left to fly out of that little hole at the bottom and make the humans regret what they were doing to her palace.

"Hey, hey!" Stef shouts now from across the table. "Don't float away on us—the night is young. Sammy! Red Bull, stat!"

Sammy climbs off the bench and scrambles to the kitchen, yanks open the fridge and tosses a blue-and-silver can across the room into his wife's waiting hands.

Stef pops it open with a hiss and thrusts it at Ruth. "Drink this."

Ruth has a headache. She massages her temples and drinks the drink.

The three girls run in from the living room then, laughing and shrieking. They're all wearing dresses for the party, exposing their bruised, bumpy knees.

"Mom!" yells Amelia. "We're hungry!"

"Keep it down!" Stef yells back.

This makes the twins shriek even louder, and Stef growls at them. "Just because you're cute doesn't mean I won't kick you in the face."

"You wouldn't kick us in the face," singsongs Isabelle, "because that would be chiiild abuuuuse."

Fern has Monsieur Foomay under her arm, and Ruth lifts her up onto her lap and kisses her hair. "No bad dreams tonight, okay?"

Fern nods and allows herself to be kissed.

Somewhere in the cottage, a machine clicks on and starts humming, promising to take care of everyone. It's a good sound, but Ruth doesn't trust it.

"Ask your father to give you some food," Stef tells the twins.

Amelia and Isabelle circle the picnic table in their fancy outfits, sequins flashing, and Amelia squeezes one eye shut and flops out her tongue. "We want to eat Fern because she's so yummy!"

"If you ate me," says Fern, "I would be poison and your guts would be dead."

"That's not nice!" says Isabelle.

"She was mean to me first," Fern grumbles.

Ruth pulls her closer and whispers, "I know."

Stef glares at Sammy. "Feed your children."

"Okay." He pulls a bag out of the cupboard and sticks it in the microwave. "Who wants popcorn for dinner?"

"Popcorn!" The twins fist-bump each other.

Fern looks up at Ruth. "Can I have popcorn for dinner too?"

"Only if you share some with me," she says, and Fern laughs.

"Look at you, all relaxed." Stef gives Ruth a dazzling smile. "I knew you'd love it here."

Ruth smiles too. "It's nice."

"I always wanted a cottage, ever since I was little." Stef picks at a corner of unmelted cheese poking out of her own burger.

"Well, you found a good place."

"To own, I mean. Not just to rent. Your mom and dad rented theirs, right?"

Ruth nods, slowly. The humidity is stifling, pressing down on her.

Fern is watching the two of them with big eyes, her fingers finding the spots she likes the best on Monsieur Foomay's wings, worn down now to a comforting softness.

"This place is probably a lot nicer than the one you went to with your parents, right? And bigger?" Stef flicks the cheese onto her plate. "I mean, I never saw it. So I wouldn't know."

The air is too still and too warm. Yesterday it was much cooler by this time. "Yes," says Ruth, "it wasn't very big." She wishes for a breeze, but there's nothing.

Then her pocket starts buzzing and jingling and she jerks around, and Fern tumbles off her lap and lands on the floor.

"Ow! Mama! Look what you did!"

Ruth reaches for her with one hand and pulls out her phone with the other, and there's James, beaming at them in miniature.

"Daddy!" Fern grabs the phone and kisses the screen.

"Hey," says Ruth, "you're going to get it all slobbery."

"Oh, let her kiss me," James admonishes from far away. "I love it."

"Fern, are you okay?" Ruth asks. "Did you hurt yourself?"

"I saw a dead fish, Daddy! And a scary movie!" Fern hops from one foot to the other. "And we're going to a fire now but it's hot so I have to be careful."

"Amazing." James's tinny laugh bubbles up, and then he pretend-pouts. "Mommy didn't say hello to me."

Fern frowns at Ruth and hands back the phone. "Say hello, Mommy."

"Hello." Ruth cradles James's face in her hands and smiles down at him. "What are you up to?"

His eyes light up. "I just watched a baby eating bacon for the first time! I'll send you the link. It'll change your life."

She shakes her head. "That's okay."

"Send it to me," Stef tells him. "You know the magic of the internet is wasted on your wife."

James sighs loudly. "Sadly, I do."

Sammy slides a giant bowl of popcorn onto the table in front of Fern, but her attention is fixed on her dad's face and she doesn't notice.

Sammy wiggles his fingers at the screen. "Hey, James."

James waves back. "Hey, Sammy."

"I'm holding down the fort, don't worry. Keeping the beers cold for you."

"I never worry when you're in charge, buddy."

"Who says I'm in charge?" Sammy wisecracks. "Just get here soon, all right? I need backup."

James chuckles. "Will do."

"How's the house coming along?" Ruth asks him. "Is everything unpacked?"

"Almost," he says.

"Give the guy a break. These things take time," Stef tells Ruth, then asks James, "How's the game coming along?"

"Almost done that too," he says.

"What game?" says Ruth.

"Just a bit of homework," Stef says quickly. "Don't worry about it. You can't actually control everything, you know. No matter how hard you try."

"I'm not trying to control anything," Ruth mutters.

"James knows what I'm talking about." Stef plucks the phone away from her and smirks at the screen. "Remember her very long list of Forbidden Pregnant-Lady Foods?"

James nods. "Oh, yes."

Ruth frowns. "It wasn't that long."

Fern climbs back onto her lap. "What are they talking about, Mama?"

"Nothing, sweetie. We're going to the bonfire soon, so you should eat some popcorn so you're not too hungry."

Fern sees the snack then and attacks it, grabbing two overflowing handfuls and quickly filling both cheeks.

"She's giving your daughter popcorn for dinner, did you hear that? The woman's come a long way." Stef starts counting on her fingers. "No deli meats, no raw fish, no unpasteurized cheeses . . ."

Ruth stiffens. "Listeria can cause a miscarriage. Why would I risk that?"

"Geez," says Stef. "So serious all of a sudden."

"All of a sudden?" James quips.

Stef grins at him and continues, "No sprouts either, but that's not a hard one to give up."

"Okay," says Ruth.

"And no alcohol, of course. I mean, I had a pint here and there with the twins and they turned out fine—more or less, ha. But *chacun à son goût*, right? The coffee ban, though." Stef shakes her head. "That was too much."

"It wasn't your baby." Ruth's voice is barely audible.

Stef finally turns away from James's face on the screen and focuses on her. "I'm still allowed to complain, aren't I?"

"Fern!" Isabelle yells from the living room. "Come and play our shooting game!"

"Okay!" She jumps off Ruth and runs to join the twins, who are huddled over their screens.

Ruth's half-eaten burger is leaking grease onto her plate. Fat is oozing out of the bites she took.

"It's just a fruit-shooting game," Stef tells her. "Nothing too dangerous."

Ruth drinks more water. "The one with the papaya guards?"

"Look at you, all technologically savvy." Stef waits until Ruth's glass is empty and then fills it with wine. "Yep. That's my and James's baby."

In the middle of taking a sip, Ruth sputters and chokes. "What did you say?"

James starts laughing again.

"Our game baby," says Stef. "The first one we ever worked on together. Relax." She pats Ruth's hand, which is shaking slightly, then lowers her voice. "Wait until you see our newest creation, though. It's the best one yet. We couldn't tell you before because Fern was listening."

Ruth frowns. "What are you talking about?"

"That's how your handsome hubby earned the big raise I gave him. He's been working very, very hard." Stef hands her the phone.

Ruth looks at James, who is grinning at her from his big desk that holds his big computer in the big home office of their big, new house. "It's for her birthday," he stage-whispers. "There's a dragon in it. She's going to lose her mind."

"Oh." The phone is heavy in her hand and the glass is so smooth. Slippery. She loosens her grip but only a little because she doesn't want to drop it. James keeps telling her to get a protective case for it but she never remembers. So it's still very fragile and could break very easily.

"Have fun at your bonfire," he says. "I'd better let you go."

"Okay," she says in a monotone. She wonders if he can hear the flatness of her voice, but probably not.

"I'll see you soon, Ruthie."

"Okay," she says again, and then he's gone.

AFTER DINNER, STEF locks up the cottage, and the six of them troop across the front lawn toward the path that will take them to Marvin and Lesley's place.

"So who else is going to this thing?" Ruth asks.

"Everybody goes," says Sammy. "Like I said, Marvin's bonfires are epic."

"You said they were legendary," says Stef.

Sammy swats a hand at her. "Whatever."

The forest closes in on them as soon as they step off the edge of the property.

"Get off my property!" Ruth used to shout at Stef when they were kids and Stef had overstayed her welcome again. Stef always treated it like a joke, but Ruth usually meant it by then.

Because it felt like Stef never left. Her parents wouldn't come to pick her up until after both girls had fallen asleep in Ruth's room, entwined on Ruth's twin bed. And then Ruth's mom would come in, saying, "Hush, it's okay, they're here now, it's time to go home, sweetie." And Stef would stumble drowsily out of bed, and through half-closed eyes, Ruth would watch her mom steering Stef away. Her friend would ask, "Were they working again?" And Ruth's mom would answer, "Yes, that's right. They work very hard, don't they?" And Stef would say, "I never want to work that hard."

Once in a while, they wouldn't pick Stef up at all, so Ruth would wake up in the morning with her friend's bad breath in her face, and they'd have to eat breakfast together and go to school together and spend all day there together too, until the bell rang and Ruth hoped and hoped that Stef's parents would be there, smiling with open arms, so Ruth could finally get a break.

The sun has just started to set and everything is orange.

Ruth says, "So I guess we'll meet Lesley, then?"

"Maybe, maybe not," says Stef. "Depends on what mood she's in. Sometimes she likes to see all the kids and sometimes she doesn't like to see all the kids."

"Oh." Ruth is holding Fern's hand tightly.

The woods claw at them from all sides. The mothers and

the father and their daughters follow the path in front of them, swatting at bugs and shoving branches away from their faces. They walk and walk, and after a while, the path narrows and the forest starts to feel different. More alive. Heat and itch and unfamiliar noises all around them, demanding constant vigilance.

"Are we going the right way?" Ruth asks.

"I know the way," says Stef, a few paces ahead. "Don't worry about it."

"Don't worry, don't worry," says Ruth, and the words startle her. The mocking tone of them.

Stef cocks her head to the side. "What did you say?"

A weak laugh trickles out. "Nothing."

"Really?"

"Hey, kids!" Sammy hustles Amelia and Isabelle and Fern farther ahead, pointing at something on the ground. "Look at all this moss—it's like nature's carpet!"

Stef stares back at Ruth. "I'm just trying to help you chill out. Because we're supposed to be having a good time."

Ruth takes a shaky breath. Her anger isn't new, but the strength of it is. The way it rushes through her, making every nerve stand at attention. "You don't have a care in the world, do you?" she says to her friend's back. "You don't even know what worries are."

Stef tenses, but keeps walking. "Don't be so sure."

The anger drains away, leaving Ruth limp. She keeps going too, tripping over roots and sticks in her sandals and scraping her bare arms on the edges of unruly bushes and tall, spiky weeds. Even the blades of grass are sharp—*Which must be why they call them* blades, *aha*—and she reaches down to scratch the pink welts multiplying on her bare legs.

Stef and Sammy are wearing T-shirts too, but they've got jeans and running shoes on.

Why didn't Ruth change into jeans and running shoes? Because she is drunk.

As she and Stef catch up with the others, a twig snaps somewhere behind them and Ruth inhales sharply. "What was that?"

"A unicorn," says Sammy.

"Yay!" Fern shouts. "I love unicorns!"

"Unicorns are for babies," says Amelia, and Isabelle snickers.

Ruth says, "Can we walk a bit faster, please?"

"I packed sparklers for the girls," says Sammy.

"Yeah! Sparklers!" Amelia and Isabelle yell.

"I'll help you with yours," Ruth tells Fern.

"She'll be fine," says Stef. "Let her have some fun."

"I just want her to be safe." Ruth frowns. "Sparklers can be dangerous."

"I don't want a sparkler!" says Fern.

"Don't listen to your mother," says Stef. "We love her, but she gets a little goofy sometimes."

"Yeah." Fern giggles. "Goofy."

"Hey!" Ruth squeezes her daughter's hand, smiling.

If James were here, he'd let Fern have a sparkler.

Stef hip-checks Sammy. "Did you pack fun things for the grown-ups too?"

"Who did you marry?" he asks her.

"Do we have flashlights?" says Ruth. "To get back?"

"Locked and loaded," says Sammy.

"Can I have one?"

"Chill, my dear, they're all in here." He pats his bulging cooler bag.

"Just give her one," says Stef. "It's getting dark."

"Yes, ma'am." He digs a small flashlight out of his bag and hands it to Ruth, and she tucks it into the backpack.

Stef watches her. "Doesn't that thing get heavy?"

"No," Ruth lies.

"Let's play hide-and-seek!" shouts Isabelle.

"Hmm," says Ruth, "I don't think that's a very good idea."

Stef snorts. "Of course you don't."

A mosquito is whining in Ruth's ear. She swats at it and misses. Then it zeroes in on Fern, diving toward her neck. Ruth smacks her hands together, then opens them to reveal the mangled bug inside.

141

"Whoa," Fern marvels. "You hit him so hard that his legs fell off."

"Okay, everybody," shouts Stef, "Auntie Ruth is going to count and we're all going to hide!"

Ruth grips her daughter's hand and shakes her head. There is no way she's losing sight of her in here. Even when they play hide-and-seek at home, Ruth will cheat. Fern will tell her to close her eyes, and Ruth will always peek through her fingers. And Fern can never understand how her mother is able to find her, every single time.

"Fine, I'll count." Stef makes a show of squeezing her eyes shut, then places her hands over her face for good measure. "One . . . two . . . three . . ."

Sammy and the twins take off running, flying away in different directions.

Fern tugs on Ruth's hand. "Mama! Let's go!"

She allows her daughter to pull her into the bushes. They find a hulking, grey trunk and crouch down behind it.

Dying sunshine filters through the trees, pulsing light and dark all around them.

"The forest is a bit spooky," Fern says quietly.

"You know what?" says Ruth. "I think it's a bit spooky too." And immediately she thinks, *Stupid.* "I mean, mostly forests are happy places. The trees give us shade so we don't get a sunburn."

"But not at night," says Fern. "At night it's a monster's house."

"Ten!" calls Stef, and Fern puts a finger to her lips. Making sure Ruth doesn't open her big mouth and ruin everything.

"You guys are good," Stef says from somewhere far away. "I'll give you that."

Fern huddles closer to Ruth and whispers, "Don't let her find us, Mama."

Minutes pass, and then Stef trumpets an "Aha!" and one of the twins squeals.

"I've already got Isabelle!" Stef crows. "So the rest of you better start worrying!"

There is a rustling behind Ruth and Fern and the two of them cringe away from the sound. Then Ruth's phone starts buzzing and she answers it fast without checking the display. "Hello?"

"Hi, Ruthie." It's her mother, and her voice is still sad.

Ruth feels a rush of guilt for not calling her back. "Hi, Mom."

"Why are you whispering?"

Fern grabs the phone and presses it against her ear. "Hi, Grandma! We're playing hide-and-seek!"

Ruth wraps an arm around her daughter. "Shh."

"I have to be quiet. Here's Mommy." Fern gives the phone back to Ruth.

"Should I let you go?" her mother asks.

"No, it's fine. We're just playing a game."

"Oh. I won't keep you, then."

There is silence between them, and then Ruth asks, "Are you okay, Mom?"

"I'm all right. I'm just thinking about him, that's all."

"I know. Me too."

Her mother sighs. "The summer is hard on both of us now, isn't it?"

Ruth doesn't answer, and her mother's voice brightens a little. "Is the cottage nice?"

"It's really nice. It's big."

"That's good. Stef deserves a nice place. Did you tell her I said hello? It's been so long since I've talked to her."

143

Not very far away, there's a scuffle and a crash and then a yowl from Sammy.

"Got you!" Stef gloats.

"I told her." Ruth clears her throat. "I guess I should probably—"

"Of course, honey. I'll talk to you another time."

"Bye, Mom." She hangs up and slides the phone back into her shorts pocket.

Fern looks up at her. "Why are you sad, Mama?"

Ruth's eyes prickle and she squeezes them shut to force the tears away. "I'm not sad, sweetie."

"Yes, you are." Fern leans against her and whispers, "I wish I got to meet your daddy."

A tiny sob escapes before she can stop it. "I wish that too."

They hold on to each other and then a twig snaps under Fern's pink sneaker and suddenly Stef is there with Isabelle, jabbing a finger at them. Claiming her next victory.

Then there's a bigger rustling from the bushes and all four of them scream and jump, and Sammy runs out, baring his teeth and growling.

"Okay." Stef crosses her arms. "Now where's Amelia?"

"She told me she knew a good spot," says Isabelle. "Where you'll never, ever find her."

"She doesn't know who she's up against," Stef says, and charges into the woods.

Ruth and Fern and Sammy and Isabelle stand still, listening.

There are invisible birds everywhere. They warble from somewhere up high, revealing themselves every so often when one or two swoop overhead, switching branches for a change of scenery.

144

The temperature is starting to drop, slowly, but the humidity is relentless tonight. Everything here is too close, too much. If Ruth knew what poison ivy looked like, she'd be watching out for it. But she doesn't, so she just pulls Fern against her and listens for animal noises.

The shadows have lengthened in the dimming light and the shapes around them are less defined now, obscured by the growing darkness. There's a big, rotting tree stump to their left—Ruth knows it's only a tree stump—but as dusk falls, it wavers. She blinks and it's a wolf, hackles raised, ready to tear them all apart.

In the distance, Stef is calling Amelia's name and zigzagging through the trees, heedless of all the delicate living things she must be crushing underfoot.

Ruth waits for the roar Amelia will release when she's discovered, but it doesn't come.

Eventually Stef stumbles back to them. "I can't find her." She's out of breath, wheezing. "I looked everywhere."

"Told you," says Isabelle.

"Isabelle." Sammy's voice is hard. "Do you know where your sister is?"

She looks at the ground. "No," she mumbles.

"Fuck." Stef runs a hand through her messy hair. Her arms are covered in scratches. "Where did she go?" She peers around them. "Goddammit, I don't know where we are."

"Are you fucking kidding me?" says Sammy.

"Jesus, Sammy," she says, "don't swear in front of the kids!"

The forest crowds in around them. Tall trees and fallen logs and plants of all sizes coiled over and under, swaying and dangling and grasping.

"We need to get back on the path," says Ruth.

Her friend stares her down. "Do *you* know where the path is?"

She points vaguely behind them. "Over there, maybe?"

Stef growls in frustration. A tear slides down her cheek and she swipes it away angrily.

"Mama," says Fern, "are we lost?"

"No, honey," says Ruth. "But Amelia is, and we need to find her." She looks at Stef. "I think we should split up."

"She's right," says Sammy. "We'll cover more ground that way."

Stef nods reluctantly.

The mothers take their daughters' hands and set off in opposite directions, and Sammy trails behind, all of them calling Amelia's name.

It's much darker now, and Ruth pulls the flashlight out of her backpack and trains the narrow beam ahead of her and Fern, shining it at the shifting woods.

On either side of them, two other flashlight beams bounce erratically, slicing through the gloom. As all five of them crash through the brush, the combined thudding and crackling from their clumsy footfalls is amplified, and then fades away.

145

The silence that follows is so startling that Ruth jolts to a standstill, halting Fern as well. She looks over her shoulder, searching for signs of the others, but the trees have devoured them completely.

And then Ruth hears something else.

"Why did we stop, Mama?"

"Shh. Just listen."

Somewhere off to her left, or maybe it's her right, she thinks she can hear crying. She starts moving again, tugging Fern along, following the sound and wondering if Stef hears it too.

Her friend has always been proud of the fact that she isn't maternal. When the twins were infants and Ruth was visiting, she always noticed their cries before Stef did. Stef used to joke that she had selective hearing. "Because they always *need* me for something," she'd say. "'Give us food. Clean the filth off of us. Don't let us die.' It's too much." And Ruth would hold her friend's beautiful babies in her empty arms and laugh like she was expected to.

The crying gets louder, so Ruth keeps moving in the same direction, pulling Fern along with her until they're far ahead. "Amelia!" she calls, over and over, until there she is.

Stef's little girl is sobbing on the forest floor next to a small something—it's not clear to Ruth at first what it is, but then the glare of the flashlight illuminates a furry mass, and then the eyes, squeezed shut in their dark mask. "Oh, honey," she says. "What did you do?"

Amelia sniffles. "I found it and it was sick."

Fern creeps closer. "What happened, Mama?"

"Don't look," Ruth tells her, and Fern reaches up and covers her face with splayed fingers.

"I was just trying to help it breathe," Amelia says. "I took a stick and made a hole where the lungs are. Because it was having trouble. I thought maybe it swallowed something bad."

Bile rises up Ruth's throat, a drowning wave of thick, black poison, but she forces it back down. "Yes," she says, "sometimes that happens."

"And then there's nothing you can do." Amelia shakes her head forlornly. "No matter how hard you try."

"You're right," says Ruth. "There's nothing."

The birds chirp and caw at the three of them, the calls coming faster and louder until they sound almost mechanical. The beeps of machines, signalling something bad.

Ruth says, "When I was a little girl, I found a clam after a seagull smashed it on some rocks."

Amelia looks up at her, away from the raccoon, and Fern whispers, "Why did the seagull do that?"

"Because it needed to break the hard shell to eat the soft body inside," Ruth tells her daughter. "Animals in the wild have to eat each other sometimes, to survive."

"I know about that." Amelia wipes her nose, smearing her cheek with pink. "I know about animals because I'm going to be a veterinarian when I grow up."

"Okay," Ruth says, trying not to show anything but kindness, "so what's the prognosis?"

Amelia frowns. "What does that mean?"

"It means what's going to happen."

"Oh." The little girl looks at the small pile of fur, which is still moving slightly. Panting, but very slowly. "I think it's going to die."

Ruth nods. "I think so too."

From far off but coming closer, Stef's voice rings out. Shouting Amelia's name.

"She's here!" Ruth calls back.

Amelia starts to cry harder, and Fern takes a few tentative steps forward and pats her awkwardly on the head.

There are ferns everywhere, so many of them. Their lacy fronds nodding in the breeze, their bright green fading as the night rolls in.

Before Fern, Ruth and James had never been able to agree on baby names.

But one day, Ruth found "Fern" on a list in a book she took out of the library. She'd always been scornful of names that were inspired by natural things, but this one felt right. And it was different from all the others.

And then Stef is there. She shrieks and runs over, leaving Isabelle with Sammy and falling to her knees in front of their other daughter. She grabs Amelia's small, trembling arms and holds on tight. "Are you okay?"

Amelia's breath hitches, and she manages a tearful nod.

Stef sees the raccoon and her eyes widen. "What the hell is that?"

"It was already hurt," Ruth says. "She was just trying to do something good."

"But it didn't work, Mommy," Amelia sobs. "I tried but it didn't work."

"Oh, sweetie." Stef clings to her, staring at Ruth over her daughter's heaving shoulders. "Mommy knows."

Ruth looks away, and sees the path through the gloom. Just beyond their little clearing. Close by the whole time but hiding too, waiting for them to find it again.

Isabelle tiptoes closer. "Is it a baby?"

"Yep," says Sammy. "The mother probably pushed it out of the nest for being bad."

"*Daddy*." Stef shoots him a warning look.

"You have to help it now." Fern's voice is hard. "Because it's in pain."

And Ruth realizes she's been watching all along.

"She's right," says Sammy. "Why don't you guys walk ahead and I'll take care of it."

Stef and Ruth usher the girls away, back onto the trail to Marvin and Lesley's place, and they all start walking.

Before they get too far, Ruth looks over her shoulder.

In the shadows of the trees, Sammy steps forward and stomps down, and the raccoon is finally still.

149

SEVEN

THE SUMMER IS JUST STARTING, AND THE MOTHER-TO-BE IS walking along the sidewalk with her giant belly floating in front of her like a beautiful balloon. She's holding on to it, rubbing circles into it.

She's tired because she's forgotten how to sleep. Her baby has stolen that knowledge from her, but the mother-to-be doesn't care.

"The doctor says you're supposed to rest," the father-to-be keeps chiding her. "Just lie down and close your eyes. It's easy."

But she'd rather spend her time waiting to feel the gentle knock-knocking that lets her know she isn't alone in her body. ("I'm here, Mama.") And when she doesn't feel it, she stings with need, desperate for her unborn daughter's entrancing company.

Because she's found a new fellow adventurer and she wants to tell her all about the weird, wonderful world she's going to live in. Because she's found a new audience and she wants to delight her with endless performances. And it's awful when she doesn't pay attention.

As soon as the knocking stops, every inch of the mother-to-be is on fire, itching for a hit of reassurance. *Please, just for a little while longer.* But when it begins again, she's ready.

She likes to sing to the baby. Mostly she revisits and revises the anthems of her wild and carefree university days, her misspent nineties youth: "Here you are now, I'll entertain you!" She goofs around with the lyrics because everything has a different meaning now: "*Today* is gonna be the *day* that we're gonna look at birds and squirrels."

She tries to explain how that music made her feel back then and how she feels when she hears it now. But the problem is, the baby inevitably falls back to sleep and the mother-to-be loses her again.

"Please stay," she whispers. "Come back. It's been seven minutes but feels like days since you took your love away."

All around them, the trees and flowers are in bright, astonishing bloom, and their branches are full of happy birds.

A man is approaching. He's not very old, maybe in his early thirties. He's one of those men who looks like a lot of men do—short hair, jeans and a T-shirt, hair on his arms.

She smiles at him because she smiles at everyone now. The baby inside her has made her all-powerful, and that power has made her benevolent toward all living things.

But the man doesn't smile back. His hands are in his pockets and he walks along like that, casually but purposefully, with jaunty elbows and an unsmiling face.

Her steps falter as he gets closer. Because now it's obvious. He's a Bad Stranger, and he's going to hurt them.

It gets darker then. A cloud covers the sun and the mother-to-be is all alone on the street with the man. There's no one else around and nowhere she can run to for help. As if she could even run. The trees are grey and the birds are screaming and it's just the two of them. The three of them.

As he draws up alongside her, his mouth twists.

She gulps a breath and waits and wishes she could close her eyes but she won't, she can't, because she has to be ready for whatever he's going to do.

And then he spits on her.

That's all.

The fat, glistening glob lands smack in the centre of her big, round belly. She is wearing a gauzy maternity top and can already feel the wetness spreading through the thin material. Some of his phlegm and saliva sprays onto her chest and chin as well, and her hands fly up to wipe it off.

His face goes blank after that and he continues on his way, but she stops and turns around. Calls out, "Hey!" before she even has a chance to think about it.

Then she thinks, *That was stupid of me.*

She waits for him to stop and turn around too. Waits for him to come back and punch her in the belly, then push her down and kick it, make a dent or cave it all the way in like a rotten pumpkin.

But he just keeps on walking.

She's still wet with his spit. The yellow glob on the curve of her middle oozes down, and she doesn't do anything about it. All of his disgust is concentrated there, and she concentrates on how it feels.

She stands there in the sunshine until the man is out of sight, the birds chirping a merry tune the whole time.

The mother-to-be thinks, *I have been cursed.*

And right then, the baby moves inside her, kicks her harder than she's ever kicked before.

And she knows that it's true.

EIGHT

UP AHEAD, THE ORANGE GLOW FLARES BRIGHTER AS THE night descends around them.

"Wow," says Ruth, "that's a big fire."

"What did I tell you?" says Sammy.

Then almost immediately, like a switch has been yanked, their voices are drowned out by shouts and hoots, clapping, laughter, cheers, competing music being played, bottles clinking. And suddenly they're in the middle of it, and there is the biggest bonfire Ruth has ever seen and the flames are raging and she thinks, *Careful, careful.*

Sammy heaves the cooler bag off his shoulder and plunks it down just a few feet away from the firepit. "Looks like a good spot right here."

"Aren't we too close?" says Ruth. "It's a bit warm."

He drags an empty camping chair over and settles into it. "It'll be cold later."

Then there is Marvin, striding toward them with a fistful of sticks and a large bag of marshmallows balanced on his head.

He reminds Ruth of the poster Stef gave her when they were kids, showing a sad Saint Bernard puppy with an old-fashioned ice pack balanced between his floppy ears. In the background was a majestic mountain, and at the bottom was a cheery slogan spelled out in rainbow colours: "When life gets you down, your friends will lift you up to new heights!" It was supposed to be inspiring, but the dog looked so depressed and Ruth couldn't help him, so it just made her feel hopeless.

"Now," says Marvin, "where are my official roasters?"

"Me! Me!" the twins yowl.

"Well, now. Don't you look nice? You got all dressed up for my party." He smiles and starts to hand a stick to Amelia, then pulls it back. "Hey, wait a minute. What are you going to give me for it?"

The little girl giggles. "A kiss?"

Ruth rests her hands on Fern's shoulders.

Marvin scrunches up his face. "Just one teeny kiss? That's all you're going to give me?"

Isabelle sidles up. "How about *two* kisses?"

"Ah," says Marvin. "Now you're talking." He crouches down in front of them and juts out his chin, and the twins plant kisses on his stubbly cheeks.

"Ow! Too scratchy!" they yell, and snatch their sticks from him.

Ruth's heart is thumping and she looks at Stef and Sammy but they're laughing, and Stef catches her eye and mouths, "Harmless."

The bag of marshmallows slides off Marvin's head but he catches it just in time, and offers it to Fern. "What about you, little one?"

Ruth pulls her closer.

Fern regards him sternly and leans back against her mother. "You're a stranger."

"But you met me already!"

"I met you yesterday," she says. "That was not a very long time ago."

Marvin laughs. "You're very smart." He smiles up at Ruth. The sharks on his shorts are swimming in all directions, and he's wearing a Hawaiian shirt. "Why don't we ask your mommy what she thinks?"

Ruth's face goes hot. *From the fire*, she thinks. "It's okay, Fern." The words creak out of her. "Marvin is our friend now, so you can have the marshmallows."

Marvin gives the bag to Fern.

She squeezes it a few times, then holds it up to her face and peers through the clear plastic.

"Please don't tell me that the child has never had marshmallows before," says Stef.

"Of course she has." Ruth smiles tightly at her daughter. "Right, honey?"

Fern furrows her brow. "I don't remember."

Stef cackles, then turns to Marvin. "We need to use your bathroom."

"Be my guest." He winks. "The outhouse is prepped and ready for use."

Stef shakes her head. "It's too dark in there. I need light to wash the raccoon blood off my daughter. Don't ask."

Marvin grimaces, then glances back at his cottage, which is dark except for a faint yellow glimmer coming from the front room and one small upstairs window.

"I don't want to wash my hands!" Amelia yells.

"There's hand sanitizer," he says quickly. "I just filled it up."

"Sanitizer's not going to cut it," says Stef. "We need actual soap and water."

"Just use the sanitizer," Sammy groans. "I want to start

drinking. And why do you care so much about our children's hygiene all of a sudden?"

Stef glares at him.

"The place is a mess," Marvin says.

"Don't worry." Stef grins. "We won't judge."

"All right." He sighs. "Follow me."

"I want to go with Amelia and Isabelle," Fern tells Ruth. So they follow Marvin too.

On the way, Stef leans close to Ruth and whispers, "I just want to see inside. They never invite us in."

"I'll be out here if you need me," Sammy calls after them. "But you probably won't."

"JESUS," STEF SAYS when Marvin lets them into his cottage, "you call this a mess?"

He shrugs. "I'd like to take credit, but Lesley does all the upkeep. She did all the decorating too."

Stef and Isabelle and Amelia and Ruth and Fern stand in the foyer, gazing around them.

The place is beautiful and immaculate. Open concept, with shiny blonde hardwood and soaring ceilings. Pale-yellow walls and numerous vases filled with fresh flowers, which Ruth never bothers with because it's such a pain to throw them away when they die.

In the centre of the living room is a sprawling, turquoise couch with fluffy, matching pillows, and a luminous green coffee table—one of those repurposed vintage steamer trunks that Ruth has always coveted but has been too lazy to ever go out and find. A small potted plant has been placed on top of it, perfectly centred.

158

The kitchen is clean and modern, with bright white cupboards. In the dining room, an enormous solid-oak table is surrounded by solid-oak chairs, all curved lines and smooth surfaces.

The tall windows are framed by gauzy, white curtains that probably look lovely when they billow in the breeze, but right now the windows are all shut tight.

Marvin sees Ruth looking at them and says, "I'd like to get some air in here, but Lesley doesn't like to smell the smoke."

"Where is Lesley, anyway?" Stef asks.

"Somewhere," he says, and crouches next to the three kids.

Fern is gripping Monsieur Foomay, recently extracted from the backpack, and Marvin pokes the dragon's soft belly. "And who might this be?"

Too close. Ruth reaches down and grasps Fern's shoulder.

"Monsieur Foomay," Fern answers solemnly.

"That's very original," he says. "Where did that name come from?"

"Auntie Stef says it's because of the smoke from his fiery breath. And he's French."

Marvin barks out a laugh. "I've got something for you, Princess Fern."

"Hey, what about us?" Amelia whines.

He frowns at her. "What did you do to the raccoon?"

"Nothing!" she shrieks. "I was trying to *help*!"

"I'm not a princess." Fern crosses her arms. "I'm the commander."

"Ha!" says Marvin. "So you are." He reaches over, his big hand moving toward her small face.

Fern's eyes go wide.

Marvin raps his knuckles very gently on her forehead. Once, twice. "Knock, knock."

159

She squirms and giggles. "Who's there?"

"Canoe."

"Canoe who?"

"Canoe come out and play with me?"

"That's a good one," says Fern. "He's funny, Mama."

Ruth nods, and lets her go.

So many of the men she's known have been jokers. Her father, James, Sammy. Even the strangers she meets are funny, most of the time.

"This place is sweet," says Stef. "Give us the grand tour!"

Marvin points to a nearby door. "There's a bathroom right there."

"Super. Now let's see the rest of it."

He stands there, head tilted to the side.

"What?" Then, "Handwashing! Right." Stef grabs Amelia by the wrist and tugs her over to the bathroom, where they disappear briefly and then come back out. "All done. What's upstairs?"

Marvin rolls his eyes. "Follow me."

The twins whisper together, and Isabelle announces, "We want to play down here."

Stef glances at Marvin, who nods. "Fine," she says. "But don't break anything."

"Hide-and-seek!" shouts Isabelle. "Fern is it!"

Fern immediately drops Monsieur Foomay so she can cover her eyes and start counting, but the twins don't take off running just yet. They hover close to her, giggling.

The adults start climbing the stairs and Ruth calls, "Mommy will be right back!"

Fern doesn't reply. She just keeps yelling out numbers, and Amelia orders, "Count higher!" So she does.

When they get to the top, Marvin leads Ruth and Stef down a long hallway. He points out a simple but homey guest-room and says, "Still unused!"

They pass a bathroom with pristine white tiles, streak-free mirrors and a gleaming-white sink and toilet.

The floor creaks under their feet but the sound is muffled by the thick, white carpet. Their shadows press against the plain, white walls.

They stop at another open doorway and Marvin mutters, "Master bedroom."

He flicks a hand to indicate the giant four-poster bed, neatly made up with a white duvet and several lace-trimmed pillows of varying sizes and colours, with a baby doll nestled in the centre of them. "That's Lesley's," he says quickly. "From when she was a kid."

161

"Cute." Stef smirks.

You had your cat, Ruth wants to say, but stays quiet.

At the end of the hall is one more room, but the door is closed.

"What's in there?" says Stef.

"It's private," says Marvin. "Let's go back downstairs."

She leans toward Ruth and murmurs, "Sex dungeon. Definitely."

Now Ruth is supposed to laugh, but she doesn't feel like it. She's so tired of her friend's voice in her ear.

Marvin stands there, blocking the way to the closed door, waiting for them to turn back. He looks smaller somehow. He's been shrinking since he started the tour, folding in on himself.

Stef makes a sudden, exaggerated move to dodge past him, flashing a gleefully disobedient grin.

And then he's a giant again, rising up and filling the space around him, his deep voice brimming with warning. "No."

The word echoes in the quiet cottage. There are no other sounds. No distant shouts of partiers by the bonfire, because all the windows are closed. No playful noises floating up from the living room, either.

Stef freezes and holds up her hands. "All right, all right."

They turn around and walk back to the staircase and start down the steps. Stef is first, Ruth is in the middle, and Marvin is last.

Below them, Fern is still hunting for Isabelle and Amelia. She's trying to be silent and so are they.

From her vantage point halfway down the stairs, Ruth can see the twins huddled behind the turquoise couch. She could point them out, but that would be cheating.

Fern keeps on looking in all the wrong places.

"Fern!" Stef stage-whispers. "Over there!"

Ruth stares at her friend's back and imagines how it would feel to push her. It would be so easy. Her arms tingle at her sides but she keeps them still.

"Ha!" Fern jumps behind the couch, jabbing a finger triumphantly. "Got you!"

The sisters blast her with outraged screams and then Amelia stands up with her hands on her hips and says, "Bet you can't find your dumb dragon, though!"

"What?" Understanding dawns on Fern, and she pales. "Mama, where's Monsieur Foomay?"

"I don't know." Ruth is at the bottom now, stepping off the last stair. "I thought he was with you."

Fern shakes her head fast. "I put him down so he could rest."

Isabelle smirks. "He wanted to play too."

Fern starts to cry. "Where is he?"

"You have to look!" says Amelia.

"Girls," says Ruth. "Get him for her, please."

The twins give her identical looks of disdain.

"You're not the boss of us," Isabelle says, sticky-sweetly.

"Isabelle and Amelia," Stef says evenly. "Give the dragon back to Fern. Now."

"Not *yet!*" Amelia shouts.

"Whatever." Stef raises her hands in surrender. "I tried." She walks over to Marvin and Lesley's kitchen and starts opening cupboards, rummaging around inside. "Where do you keep your food, Marvin? I'm starvin'."

He looks haggard all of a sudden, and slumps onto one of the dining-room chairs without answering her.

Fern starts running, peeking into corners and under furniture.

Ruth searches too.

Stef says, "Aha!" and holds up a bag of potato chips.

"Give me some of those," Marvin mumbles.

"Us too!" The twins scurry to their mother and start pawing at the bag.

"They're barbecue!" Stef tells them. "You don't like that kind!"

But they keep begging, so she finds a small bowl and fills it for them with a snarl.

Amelia and Isabelle rush back to the living room without a thank-you and perch side by side on the couch with the chips between them, watching Fern with mean, orange smiles.

"Where is he?" Fern shrieks at them. "Tell me!" Tears and snot stream down her red face.

"Maybe you'll never find him," Amelia singsongs.

"Maybe he's gone forever!" Isabelle trills.

163

"Don't worry, honey," says Ruth. "I'll help you find him."

But Fern ignores her. Her eyes narrow and she charges at the twins. "Give him to me!"

She leaps onto the couch and starts pummelling them, and all three girls become a howling, whirling blur of hair and skin and teeth. The chips fly everywhere, and the bowl lands on the floor with a dull thud.

"Stop it," says Ruth. But no one is listening to her.

And then a child's foot—it's impossible to tell whose—kicks out and knocks the perfectly centred potted plant off the coffee table and onto the wood floor with a crash. Then the three girls break apart at last, gazing around in wonder for the source of the loud noise. A glowing-red scratch spans the width of Amelia's chin, and Isabelle's bottom lip is bleeding. Fern doesn't have a mark on her.

Marvin stands up and observes the cushions on the floor, the spilled chips and the broken pieces of ceramic mixed into the pile of dirt and helpless green leaves.

When they were kids, Stef made so many messes at Ruth's parents' house over the years, and Ruth always had to tidy them up after Stef left. "We know it's not fair, honey," her mom and dad would tell her. "But it's easier this way, okay?"

If something was broken, though, they would take care of it. They'd sweep up the pieces of whatever Stef had smashed, and Ruth would stand at the front window while Stef's parents' car drove away. Sometimes her friend would be watching her from the back seat and Ruth wouldn't even wave, and her parents would just keep sweeping because they didn't want Ruth to get hurt.

Except one time, early on, when Ruth and Stef were six years old and Stef picked up Ruth's mom's special flower vase and threw it on the floor. It broke into a million pieces and there was water everywhere and the flowers were drowning in it, and Ruth yelled at Stef and said she was bad. Ruth's mom ran into the dining room then and grabbed Ruth's arm, and suddenly her hand was a monster hand and she pulled Ruth away from Stef and into the kitchen, where she grew ten sizes taller and had long claws and sharp teeth and giant black wings, and she hunched down and hissed in a deep, scary voice with awful, stinky breath in Ruth's face, "Don't you ever tell her she's bad. Do you hear me? Don't you ever tell her she's bad because she's not, and nobody even cares if she's good or bad at home anyway. This is a happy place for her here and I will not allow you ruin it. Do you understand?"

Ruth was crying and shaking but her mother wouldn't stop and turn back into herself. Her voice deepened even more and she growled, "Nod if you understand me."

So Ruth nodded to make her mom nice again, and it worked. The claws disappeared and the wings folded in on themselves and the teeth were flat and white instead of pointy and yellow, and her face was kind again and she was just Ruth's mom who loved her. She leaned in and wrapped Ruth in a hug and her breath was sweet when she said, "That's my good girl. Now go and play with your friend and tell her you're sorry. Mommy and Daddy will clean everything up later, don't worry."

Now the twins each take one of Fern's hands, their fight forgotten, and lead her to the green coffee table. They heave the heavy chest open, excited to show their friend what they've done.

Ruth can't help but admire their stealth. They must've hidden Fern's toy in there when nobody was looking. They would've had to lift up the potted plant and put it back too, but of course it's not there now.

Barry the treasure where no one can find it!

With grave ceremony, Amelia hands Monsieur Foomay to Fern, who makes sure to say thank you before she hugs him to her chest and presses her face into his soft scales, drying her tears and wiping her nose on his shiny wings. Because no matter how many other stuffed animals Ruth tries to ply her with, the dumb dragon will always be her daughter's favourite.

Marvin says something, too softly for anyone to hear.

And Stef says—brazenly, rudely, stupidly—"What was that?"

"I *said*, they shouldn't have done that." His big hands are clenched at his sides.

All three girls stop what they're doing and cover their ears, cowering from the anger in his deep voice.

"Marvin, stop it. You're scaring them." This voice is new. Prim and bristling, coming from above.

"Hey!" says Stef. "It's Lesley!"

A dainty woman with short, curly hair stands at the top of the stairs. She's probably in her mid-forties but looks more worn down than the rest of them. She's very thin, with sharp-looking knees that poke at the folds of her long nightgown.

"In the flesh," Marvin says, backing away slightly.

His wife scowls down at him. "Marvin, don't say things like that in front of the children."

"What, *flesh*?" he says. "Is *flesh* a bad word now?"

Lesley pulls her blue knitted cardigan more tightly around her as she glides down the steps and over to the fallen plant. Her outfit seems to belong to someone much older than she is, and larger. She picks up a piece of broken pottery, then drops it back onto the pile of dirt.

"They were hiding things in there." Marvin gestures at the open chest.

Lesley's slim hands flutter up to knead her collarbones, which jut out like wings. "Let them keep playing. It's fine."

Fern charges off with Monsieur Foomay and runs up the stairs, shouting, "It's our turn to hide!"

Lesley fidgets with her nightgown and watches Fern go. "They're always running off somewhere, aren't they? On to the next adventure." She nods over at Stef. "Hello, Stephanie. It's good to see you."

Ruth waits for Stef to apologize for the mess, but she just raises the bag of chips in greeting and says, "Hi, Lesley. You're looking well."

The twins blink around them as if waking up from a dream, and then they start jumping up and down and squealing, "Lesley! Lesley!"

She smiles at them and opens her arms wide. "Hello, my darlings."

But instead of rushing in for a hug, they run over and start grabbing at her, pulling on her slender arms and reaching into the droopy pockets of her cardigan. "What do you have for us? What do you have?"

Lesley's smile sags. There's a flash of irritation in her eyes, but then it's gone. She straightens up and digs both hands into her pockets.

Isabelle throws her head back and howls, "*What is it?*"

"Now, now." Lesley holds out two closed fists for the twins. "Guess where."

Amelia slaps the top of Lesley's right hand, and Marvin's wife winces slightly before uncurling her palm, which is empty.

"The other one! The other one!" the twins shout.

Lesley opens her left hand to reveal two candies in silver wrappers, and the twins immediately snatch and open and gobble them up, letting the wrappers drift to the floor.

Stef doesn't move to pick them up, so Ruth does. Then she lifts her hand in a feeble wave. "Hi, I'm Ruth. And that was Fern. You have a lovely place here."

"Thank you." Lesley beams at her. "We had this cottage built especially for us, did Marvin tell you? Exactly the way we wanted it. We hand-picked all the furnishings as well. It's our dream come true."

"Mama!"

Ruth jumps at her daughter's voice.

Fern is standing at the top of the stairs, clutching at the hem of her dress.

"Honey, be careful you don't fall." Ruth takes a step toward her.

Lesley stares up at Fern. "Look at her. She's beautiful." Then she frowns. "She's hiding something."

"What?" says Ruth. "What are you talking about?"

"Look at her. There's a bulge."

Oh no.

"Mama! I have a baby!" Fern pats the lump over her tummy, visible now beneath her clothes.

All the colour has bled out of Lesley's face. "What is she doing?"

"Fern," says Ruth. "That's not a good game for right now."

"Look! She's about to get born!" Fern tugs at her dress, and a plastic doll—the one from Marvin and Lesley's bed—falls out onto the carpet with a soft thump. It rolls onto the top step and then somersaults the rest of the way down, bumping to a stop at Lesley's bare feet. "I found her upstairs! Can I keep her?"

Lesley nudges the doll with her toe, then bends to pick it up. "No," she says. "She's mine."

"That's okay," says Fern. "Sometimes people don't like to share their extra-special toys, so we have to understand."

"I'm so sorry," Ruth says to Lesley in a rush.

"It's all right. It's not her fault." Lesley strokes the doll's smooth skin. "It's normal for them to test us. They pull us in and they push us away." She smiles a distant smile. "Because they know we love them when they're very, very good, but they're never sure how we'll feel when they're very, very bad."

Fern comes down the stairs slowly, and when she reaches the bottom, Lesley asks her, "Would you like a candy, sweetheart?"

Fern trembles with excitement. "Yes, please."

Lesley tucks the doll under one arm and digs another treat out of her pocket. "Look how polite you are."

"She's perfect, isn't she?" Stef picks something out of her teeth. "She's a gift from the angels."

Fern carefully unwraps her candy and holds the bright-green sweet briefly in her hand before popping it into her mouth. She stares at Lesley. "Why is your hair so curly?"

"Fern," says Ruth. "Shh."

"No, it's a fine question." Lesley bends forward and offers her head for Fern's inspection. "Would you like to guess?"

Fern looks closely at Lesley's curls. "Because it's a nest for birds?"

Lesley leans back and releases a high, breathless laugh. "Oh, that's priceless! Yes, Fern. That's exactly right. My hair is a nest for birds. But these birds are very special, do you know why?"

"Why?" Fern whispers.

"Because they're so small you can hardly even see them. Well, one of them got bigger. He was my extra-special one. But the rest of them start out being small, and they stay that small forever and ever."

Ruth gets colder as Lesley speaks, even though there's no breeze. She hugs herself and her head fills with a chorus of hushed voices, murmuring concern.

169

"How small?" says Fern. "Like a snail?"

"Smaller than a snail. Smaller than the nail on your pinky finger, right there." Lesley touches Fern's baby finger, feather-soft. "They are so small that they barely even exist, but they do. They arrive—'Hello!'—and they stay in my nest and keep me company for a while, and then they fly away. 'Goodbye!'"

Fern's giggle is uncertain. "Do you get lonely when they go?"

"I do." Lesley reaches out and clasps Fern's hands in hers. "But then I met you just now, and you made me happy again. Isn't that such a nice thing that you did?"

Instead of answering, Fern makes an odd sound, a sort of whistling. Then she puts her hands on her throat.

"Fern," says Ruth, "are you okay?"

The little girl's eyes are too wide. She shakes her head, the tiniest movement.

Ruth bolts over, reaching for her daughter. Lightning speed and useless arms. She has no idea what to do.

She squeezes her eyes shut, summoning up the friendly young woman with the long, wiggling ponytail who taught the infant-and-child first-aid course Ruth and James took when Fern was a baby, because they wanted to do everything they could to keep her safe. The woman had instructed James and Ruth and the other anxious new parents in her chirpy voice, "If your child is choking, you should first encourage him or her to cough."

"Fernie?" says Ruth. "Can you cough?"

No answer.

"Somebody do something," says Stef. "She's turning blue."

Any second now, she's going to cough.

"Marvin!" Lesley shouts. "Help her!"

Her voice jolts him into action and he leaps toward Fern. He thumps her on the back, hard, and the candy flies out of her mouth and lands on the floor with a small cracking sound that reverberates in the silent room. It lies there, glimmering like a jewel.

No one speaks until Fern coughs, wipes some drool from her chin and takes a long, ragged breath.

Ruth whispers, "Thank you," as she picks Fern up and holds on tight. Then she says, mostly to herself, "I didn't think you were supposed to hit a choking person on the back anymore. That's what they taught us in the first-aid course we took."

Lesley bends down to pick up the candy, still cradling the doll in her other arm. "You can clean up the other mess later," she tells Marvin as she heads toward the kitchen.

171

The rest of them rouse themselves, getting ready to leave.

"Whew!" Stef slaps her thighs and stands up. "Not a dull moment with this bunch, right Lesley?"

Lesley gives her a wisp of a smile. She looks even smaller now, dwarfed by the wide, blank walls and sky-high ceiling.

Marvin opens the front door and ushers everyone outside, and a few tendrils of smoke immediately reach in. "I left your tea on the counter for you," he tells his wife gently. "It's cold now, though. Sorry."

"That's all right, I don't mind. Thank you." She nods. "It was nice to meet you, Ruth and Fern."

Ruth starts to answer her, but then Marvin closes the door and she's gone.

THE BONFIRE IS much bigger now.

Ruth and Fern and Stef and Amelia and Isabelle walk toward it, leaving the cottage behind, and Marvin lopes off to greet some new arrivals.

Sammy waves to them from his camping chair, with several empty chairs around him.

There are a lot of people. Sitting, standing, dancing, tossing Frisbees and kicking balls back and forth. Eating and drinking and laughing and shouting across the vast expanse of lawn.

"I didn't realize there were so many cottages around here," Ruth says to Stef. "Your place seems so remote."

"Everybody comes from all over," says Stef. "Word gets out that Marvin's hosting, and the horde descends."

The party is wilder than Ruth was expecting. Adults talk and joke together, heedless of the many small children running around unattended, and teenagers don't bother hiding the beer and wine and liquor bottles they're passing around.

As the mothers and daughters get closer, Sammy frowns at Isabelle's bloody lip and the scratch on Amelia's chin. "What the hell happened to you two?"

Both girls point at Fern. "She did it!"

"Really?" He gives Ruth an appraising look. "That wasn't very nice."

"They were all fighting," she rushes to say, giving Fern's arm a squeeze.

"Okay, kids," says Stef. "Go play!"

Ruth leans down and whispers to Fern, "You can stay with me if you want."

But Amelia yells, "Come on, let's go!" Then Isabelle takes Fern's hand and all three girls vanish, just like that.

Ruth starts after them but Stef grabs her arm. "We'll go and find them later. Let them have some fun for now."

"I let her have fun." Ruth rises up on tiptoes, peering into the dark. "I just like to know where she is, that's all."

"I guess this whole thing is a lesson in letting go for you, right?" says Sammy.

Ruth frowns. "Excuse me?"

Stef sits down beside Sammy and whacks him on the shoulder. "Give her a break, okay? Her kid just almost choked to death."

"Shit. Is that why you guys took so long?"

"Yes," says Stef, then lowers her voice. "And they also met Lesley."

"Aha. I thought I smelled extra sugar on the girls' breath." He glances around for Marvin, making sure he's out of earshot. "So what's inside the fortress, my sneaky little snoop? I can't believe you got in there on that ridiculous pretense. Washing your child's hands, my ass."

"I know!" She grins at him. "Super fancy. Stupid clean. I couldn't see one room, though—the door was closed."

He nods. "That's where they keep the whips and chains, obviously."

"Obviously." Stef's grin widens.

"Fern's fine," Ruth tells him. "Thanks for asking."

"Ooh, touchy." Sammy aims a look at Stef and then busies himself with the cooler bag. "All I was saying, though, is that sometimes you have to love them from a distance. You have to give them some freedom or they'll just run away one day and never come back."

Someone on the other side of the bonfire pokes the coals, sending up a spray of sparks.

"I don't think that's true," says Ruth. "Not yet, anyway."

Stef rips open a package of Oreos, speaking as gently as she can. "I think what he means is, it wouldn't be so bad if you let

Fern fall off the monkey bars sometimes. It's not your job to protect her from every single awful thing in the world, and the sooner you figure that out, the happier you'll be and the stronger she'll be. It's a win-win." She pops a cookie into her mouth and chomps down.

Music is playing from somewhere. Nothing that Ruth recognizes. A woman's sad, sighing voice and a fast, insistent beat that she wouldn't know how to dance to.

"See, here's the thing." Stef's teeth are black with pulverized Oreos. "You have a skewed view of reality because Fern still thinks you're a rock star, but that won't last. You've got maybe another year, year and a half, tops. They go to school and they're gone. They have their friends and they don't need us anymore."

"They always need us," says Ruth.

"Oh yeah? Let's have this talk again when she's seven and she tells you she hates you on a regular basis. See how you feel then. You won't even care that she hates you because you'll be so fucking glad to be away from her. She can yell and scream and slam her door and you'll just be thrilled to be on the other side of it."

Ruth shakes her head. "I don't think I'll ever feel that way."

"Well, I'm happy for you. I'm happy that you two are so comfy-cozy."

Sammy reaches out to pat Stef's knee.

"You're not your parents, you know," Ruth murmurs.

"What did you say?" Her friend's eyes narrow.

"I just mean that you're better than they were, that's all. You love your kids."

Stef juts out her chin. "They love me."

Ruth nods. "I know they do."

"Not my kids."

"What?"

"I mean my parents. My mom and dad love me."

"Yes, of course. I wasn't saying—"

"It doesn't matter. I don't want to talk about this anymore." Stef thrusts a hand at Sammy, fingers waggling impatiently. "Give me a beer."

Sammy pulls a can out of the cooler bag and hands it to her as Marvin bounds back over to them, his good mood restored.

He hovers there for a moment, taking in everyone's stiff posture, and then he carefully folds himself into one of the flimsy chairs. "Grab a seat, Ruth," he says. "Get comfy."

She's the only one still standing.

"Come on, Ruthie. Take a load off." Sammy slaps the empty chair next to his. Then he pulls a joint out of his pocket and starts to light it.

"Oh, should we maybe not—when they—" Ruth squints to the left and right of the bonfire, trying to locate Fern and the twins.

Sammy raises an eyebrow at her. "It's no different than getting drunk in front of the kids. Right?"

"I never get drunk in front of Fern." Ruth squares her shoulders. "I always pace myself until she's asleep."

Sammy sucks on the joint and blows a big plume of smoke over her head. "Sure you do."

Stef holds out her arms. "Hey, hey! Calm down, everyone. Cottage Time is a magical time, when the indulgence of spirits and other substances—yes, some of them are still illegal in some parts of the world, but for how much longer?—is not only encouraged, but mandatory. We like to think of Cottage Time as a soothing balm for Real Life."

Sammy passes Stef the joint, grinning. "I love you, babe."

175

"Right back at you, you revolting man." She takes a haul and passes it to Marvin, who holds it out to Ruth. "Ladies first."

"You should have some of that," Stef tells her. "Seriously."

"Fine. Give it here." Ruth takes the joint and finally sits down. "But I'm only having a tiny bit."

Stef claps her on the back and starts pulling more beer cans out of the cooler bag. "We can have some drinks too, if that makes you feel better."

SOME TIME LATER, not too much time but maybe a lot, Ruth realizes it's been a while since she's heard the happy shrieks that reassure her that Fern and the twins haven't disappeared forever.

Sammy and Stef aren't worried, though, so Ruth tries not to worry either. She sits back and sips her beer, and every part of her is warm and she likes the songs that keep playing, the repetitive rhythm of them. They sound like a heartbeat.

Every so often, random guests will pass by and wave at Marvin. Their smiles are tentative and respectful, but they never say anything. Sometimes he waves back and sometimes he doesn't.

Stef takes a swig of red wine from her travel mug. "Amelia punched a kid at Creative Movement last month."

"Yikes," says Marvin. "What's that?"

"Basically a bunch of seven-year-olds bounce around on gym mats like insane people for an hour. It's a total bullshit class but the parents get to sit on uncomfortable chairs and drink shitty coffee in peace so what the hell. Anyway, the kid punched her back and then the kid's mother and I started shoving each other and long story short, my family is banned from Creative Movement for all eternity, which is actually a fucking blessing if you ask me, but it still doesn't feel good, you know? Then before we left, Isabelle took a crap in the kitchen sink at the community centre, which logistically, how did she do that, it's pretty impressive, and in my heart I know she was doing it for me, because of us being kicked out and my pride being hurt and everything. Which was sweet of her, but also really bizarre and unsettling." She pauses to gulp some more wine. "This is why we bought the cottage. Our children are not ready for society."

"Nobody sets limits for their kids anymore," says Sammy. "Kids need boundaries. If we didn't lock the twins in a closet once in a while and turn off the light and say there was a monster in there with them, they wouldn't listen to us at all."

"That's only if they're really being fuckers, though," Stef adds.

Marvin says, "Better a kid who doesn't listen than no kid at all, right?"

Sammy smacks himself on the forehead. "Jesus, Marvin, I'm sorry. I didn't mean—"

"No, it's okay." Marvin gives him a sad smile. "I thought Lesley might come and enjoy the fire tonight, I guess. It's a good one."

His voice vibrates in Ruth's chest, finding a home there. He and Lesley both wanted kids, she understands now, and they don't have them.

"It's a great one, buddy," says Sammy. "Your bonfires are the best."

Marvin gives him a sombre salute. "Thanks for saying that."

All around them, revellers are shouting, singing, dancing, and spearing marshmallows and hot dogs onto sharpened sticks and thrusting them into the fire.

Ruth says, "The kids are around here somewhere, right?" Trying to sound casual.

"Of course they are," says Sammy.

"They must be here. They wouldn't have gone anywhere else, would they?"

Stef lifts her travel mug to her lips and tilts it up high, emptying it all the way. "They know not to go into the woods or down to the water by themselves. Where else would they go?"

"You'd be surprised," says Marvin, and they all turn to look at him. "But I'm sure they're fine," he adds quickly.

"They're fine, right?" says Ruth. Anxiety creeping in.

Not too far away, the pointy tips of evergreens and the thinnest branches waving from the tops of the leafy trees are spotlit by the blaze. Sometimes the dark shapes of bats will flit between them, so quickly that it's hard to be sure that they were even there at all.

"They're fine." Stef shakes her head. "They're smart girls."

"Wait a minute," says Sammy, "are you talking about *our* children?"

She snorts out a laugh. "I did drink quite heavily when they were in the womb." She catches Ruth's eye. "Fern, on the other hand, is perfect. She's a gift from an angel."

"You said that already," says Marvin.

Stef shrugs. Her teeth are black again, stained by the red wine this time. "Because it's the truth."

He looks between her and Ruth, who isn't smiling. "That's nice."

Nobody speaks for a while. The fire crackles and the embers glow.

Suddenly the music changes and Stef shouts, "Holy shit, they're playing Pearl Jam! Let's go!" She jumps up and grabs Ruth's arm and drags her over to a group of dancing twenty-somethings, and Ruth lets herself be dragged.

Stef twirls her around. "Goddamn, I love this song." She throws her head back and sings along to "Better Man" at top volume, and a few of the young women around them snicker.

Stef sneers and yells, "We were your age when this came out, skanks!"

Ruth shakes her head. "You are totally going to get us beat up."

Now Stef is doing her angry dance, which involves jabbing her elbows at anybody who comes near, and Ruth does her best to run interference, shooting apologetic glances at the other dancers.

She spins around with her friend, trying to forget about everything and sink into this music that is so perfect because it reminds her of the glorious time they spent apart.

Ruth used to slip a homemade mix-tape into her Walkman and slip the bulky machine into the giant front pocket of her bulky overalls, and roam around the campus by herself listening to Pearl Jam and Nirvana and Oasis and Sinéad O'Connor. She'd belt out the lyrics and dance as she walked, twirling and shimmying and even skipping sometimes when her glee was uncontainable, even if people could see her. Nobody cared anyway. Other students would smile and give her the thumbs-up when she grooved by. They were all far from home, away from the rules of parents and the tyranny of childhood friends. Free from limits and expectations and old, destructive patterns. Free to be someone different if they wanted to, or just free to be the person they'd been all along.

Stef leans in, so close that her breath is warm on Ruth's face. "I love you, you know."

The shaggy pine and spruce branches sway all around them, black now instead of green. The leaves on the oaks and maples and elms rustle, and the scattered white birches are ghosts in the dark.

"Ha," says Ruth.

"Hey." Stef stops grinning and crosses her arms. "You didn't even notice my eye makeup."

"Oh. It looks nice."

Stef punches her arm. "Bitch."

"Ow!"

Marvin walks over with two more beers. "Ooh, can I put you two in a cage and watch you fight to the death and then I get to keep the winner?"

Before handing the cans over, he holds them up and jangles them exactly like the animated dog on *Puppy Commander* does with the owner's leash when it's time to go for a walk, and the owner immediately stops whatever he's doing and puts his hands up to his face and sticks his tongue out and pants excitedly.

Which makes Ruth wonder if Marvin has ever watched the show, but that would be silly, he doesn't have kids, and why would anyone watch that show if they didn't have kids? It's terrible.

"Marvin, I'll say it again—you're a creepy man." Stef takes a contented swig. "Mmm, delicious roofies."

Ruth stares at them.

"Drink up," says Stef. "I'm kidding, Jesus."

"Okay." Ruth heads back to her chair, but on the way there, everything swims and then she's on the ground, spilled beer foaming by her feet.

Stef reaches for her, but Ruth waves her off and rescues her half-empty can. "I'm fine."

Her friend holds up her hands. "Whatever you say." Then, "Sammy? You wanna go look for our daughters?"

Sammy finishes off his own beer and tosses the empty can behind him. "Not really."

"You wanna go make out?"

"Yes."

And just like that, before she really knows what's going on, Ruth is alone with Marvin.

"Let me help you up," he says, and this time she doesn't argue.

He lifts her under her floppy arms and deposits her in an empty chair.

"Let me do this for you. It's something I'm good at," Stef said, a long time ago.

Ruth and Stef and James were in the family room of Stef and Sammy's big house. Ruth and James were sitting together on the couch and Stef stood in front of them and took their drinks out of their hands and set them down on the coffee table next to the big bowl of chips she'd put out earlier, proclaiming this was an occasion for junk food. ("But isn't that every occasion? Ha ha.") She crossed her arms and said they had to listen to her, but they just leaned against each other and reached for their drinks again.

Sammy had already gone to bed because the one-year-old twins would be awake very early in the morning. The floor was littered with their toys and there were baby gates in every doorway.

The couch floated in the middle of the messy room, a little island for Ruth and James, and she wondered how many times he and Stef had sat together like this on the island they'd visited a few months before. They'd taken a business trip to a

181

tropical paradise and she wondered how much work they'd gotten done.

She wasn't paying attention to what Stef was saying but then her friend's voice was pleading with them, *please*, she really wanted to help because she loved them and they'd all known each other for so long, they were basically family already. This would just be one more adventure they had together, one more great story to tell, and it might be weird at first but who cared about that because at the end of it they'd have a child.

And Ruth had been about to say no, that was a generous offer but no, it wasn't a good idea. But then James started to nod. Even though Ruth kept shaking her head. Back and forth, back and forth.

Later that night when they were alone, she told him, "I'm not giving up yet."

And he said, "It's not giving up. It's just doing things differently."

"No," said Ruth. "I need one more try, before that. Just the two of us." And she kissed him, and he kissed her back, but something was missing and she didn't know what it was.

Marvin lets out a low chuckle, his grin half in shadow. "Somebody should've warned you."

"What did you say?" Ruth's thick tongue is clumsy with the words and they come out wrong. Or maybe not.

"Sammy's weed is pretty strong. Especially if you're not used to it."

"I'm fine." She gazes at the flames, trying to pick out animal shapes like her dad taught her to do when she was little. Her mom would head back to the cottage to sleep, and he and Ruth would sit around the campfire for hours. "How long have we been sitting here?"

"A while."

There's a horse, galloping.

She should get up and look for Fern but the chair is so comfortable. And she's so heavy in it.

"You want another drink?" Marvin asks her, smiling. "You spilled most of your last one."

She shakes her head but the movement is very small. Unconvincing.

At times like these when Ruth is away from her little family, it's not so much that she misses James and Fern, but that she begins to wonder if they ever existed at all. And then that possibility grows inside her and obliterates all other possibilities, so that it becomes easy to believe, and the shock of realizing it squeezes all the breath out of her at once.

"Where's Fern?" Ruth strains her eyes against the darkness, feeling a surge of hope when she spots three small forms running toward them with sparklers held high. When they get closer, though, they're somebody else's kids.

Did the girls come back and get their sparklers at some point? She struggles to remember. *Yes, they did.* When? *Before.* But who lit them? *Not me.*

There's a cat, burning.

Farther back, where there isn't so much smoke, a billion stars light up the sky. Ruth wishes she could point them out to Fern. If Fern were with her right now, that's what she would do.

"She's such a lovely little girl." Marvin's voice floats to her from far away. "I'd worry about her too."

She rubs her eyes, which are stinging from the smoke.

"Having a baby is so easy for some people. But they're not the lucky ones." His words are echoey, distorted. "Do you want to know why?"

Ruth feels herself nod. Her head is a rubber ball, bouncing.

"Because if nothing ever goes wrong along the way, you get to the end and you have your child, but you don't appreciate them. Not in the same way." He pauses and stares into the fire. "But when you have a hard time, you get to the end and you have your child, and you're grateful every day."

"I am," she says, even as she's feeling sad for this kind man who has no child at all.

"I know you are." He gives her a big smile. "Gratitude makes life better. Without it, life is just something to get through. So hold onto it, okay?"

184

"Okay," Ruth says, and she tries to picture her daughter in a situation with the best possible outcome and does her best to direct all of the negative energy away from her. Fern is fine. She'll be okay. She belongs to Ruth, and Ruth is so grateful.

She has Fern now because her arms were so empty they ached, and then she didn't have her father anymore and she was cold, and it still hurt to stand for long periods of time and she'd been standing all day, and all of the sandwiches at her dad's funeral were so ridiculously small. Stef went to get James and the two of them returned to the reception room together and walked right over to Ruth, and for a moment, Ruth thought they were holding hands, but no, of course they weren't. James was in love with Ruth. They were still together, even though they'd barely touched each other for two months because Ruth was still so sore. But she could tell he was losing patience with her. Stef said, "My offer still stands, you know," and James rested his hand on Ruth's shoulder and it was too heavy but she pretended not to notice, and this time Ruth said yes. Just the one word, out loud. It was all she could manage. She didn't have enough strength left to even complete the sentence: *Yes, carry our baby for us. I'm too tired to keep trying.*

"Don't worry," Marvin says. "The kids are safe. Everybody's got their eye out." He reaches down and opens a little cooler by his feet.

Ruth stares at it. *Where did that come from?* It must've been there all along, though, and she just didn't notice it. It's easier not to notice things all the time.

His thick fingers grip the necks of two bottles. Something red. "Here," he says. "Live a little."

She takes the bottle he hands her and presses her fingertips against the cold glass.

Marvin smiles as she unscrews the cap. "Fruit punch was his favourite."

"Who?" She's already swallowed a big mouthful. It's too sweet, but she doesn't care.

"Mine, I mean." He winks. "My favourite."

He's always winking, thinks Ruth. *That's a funny thing to do.*

Her bottle is half empty already. She's guzzling it because it's familiar. Her parents used to let her have fruit punch at the cottage. It's a little kid's drink.

All around them, pretty young women in tight pants that show off their hips are dancing with handsome young men in droopy undershirts that show off their biceps. Some of the boys are sporting furry hats shaped like animal heads, like something children would wear. It's weird, but the girls seem to think it's cute. They keep reaching up and petting the plush fox and lion and elephant heads and giggling.

Marvin stands up and holds out his hand. "So, Miss Ruth, do you still think I'm the Big Bad Wolf?"

"No," she says, "I think you're nice." The words fall out of

185

her, and she floats up and out of the chair and into his arms.

He holds on tight, smiling down at her. "Everybody's nice."

Ruth has never been this relaxed. She presses her face against Marvin's strong, broad chest just like the girls around them are pressing their faces against the boys' strong, skinny chests. She sways her hips that are rounder than the young women's hips, and watches the girls rub the boys' hard backs and the boys nip the girls' soft ears. Sometimes the girls will say, "Stop that!" But they don't really mean it.

When Stef was pregnant with Fern, she once joked that instead of sending James into a room with dirty magazines, the doctor had sent him into a room with *her*. She and Ruth were shopping for baby clothes together, and Ruth was holding a flannel sleeper. So tiny and so soft. "You're not helping," she said quietly.

And Stef rubbed the curve of her ripening belly and deadpanned, "Oh, but I *am*."

Ruth hadn't been there when the embryo was transferred. She hadn't wanted to leave her bed. But she knew the baby was hers. Made by Ruth and James, together. It was silly to believe anything else. James drove Stef to the clinic because he said it would be rude not to. He waited with her while she recovered. They were like brother and sister, and Stef was just a place for Fern to stay for a while. She wasn't her home.

Ruth pinched the tag on the sleeper and frowned at it. "I shouldn't get the newborn size, right? Because it'll be too small?"

"Yep. She'll outgrow it in a day." Stef yanked a miniature sailor suit off the rack, making the other hangers rattle. "Sammy hates that I'm doing this, by the way," she said, playing with the outfit's wide, frilly collar. It looked more like a Halloween costume than actual clothes. "He says it's not worth it." She sneered at the sailor suit and put it back. "Only an asshole would make a baby wear this."

"What are you thinking about?" Marvin asks her.

"Nothing," says Ruth.

He nods, and his chin bumps the top of her head when he does that because he's so tall. "That's all I ever think about too."

Every so often, a girl will steer her boy over to another couple and she'll tilt her head close to the other girl's, and they'll whisper to each other.

"If we do this, I know it can't be a secret," Ruth told James at home after the funeral, after they'd said goodbye to her weeping mom, when Ruth finally agreed. After her idea for one more try had turned out to be the wrong one and that baby was gone and everyone was sad, and then her dad was gone too and there was nothing left to do but say yes. "But I don't ever want to talk about it, because I don't ever want to think about it." She gave him a small smile before he could argue. "We don't talk about a lot of things," she said. "It's easy."

Suddenly there are shouts and shoving close by. "Leave me alone! You're hurting me!" A girl is yelling at a boy and the firelight makes it all seem extremely cinematic.

Ruth feels Marvin's arms wrap around her protectively and they move away.

Now the boy is yelling at the girl, which is not cool. But he's doing it and the girl is trying to pull away but he yanks her back. "Fuck off, don't be stupid," he yells at her. "There are old people here and they're watching us."

The girl shouts, "This is assault! You're assaulting me!"

And the boy says, "You shouldn't say that shit because my mom had cancer last year."

Her hands fly from her sides and up to her mouth and she

says, "Oh!" and envelops him in her bare, bruised arms. She says, "It's okay, you're okay."

He rests his zebra head on her pointy shoulder and says, "Why are these old people here, anyway?" Then he kisses her, hard. Mashes his mouth against hers and the girl squeezes her eyes shut tight, and is that blood? No, it can't be blood. Just smeared lipstick. They're only kissing. They like each other.

"You poor mothers of daughters." Marvin shakes his head sadly. "You have to be very vigilant, don't you?"

Fern.

Ruth unwinds herself from Marvin, every part of her coiled up tight.

Shreds of laughter reach them from the other side of the fire and she squints at another couple dancing by the flames, farther away. The woman is leaning her head on the man's shoulder. Ruth can only see their backs, but she knows who they are.

Why didn't he tell me he was here?

Because he wanted to see her first.

She takes a few steps toward them and calls out, "Hey!"

But they just keep dancing.

She waits for them to stop and turn around. She waits for them to see her and run over and feel guilty and apologize.

"Ruth?" says Marvin. "Are you okay?"

"Hey!" she yells again, and this time they swivel to face her, frowning.

Just two strangers. She doesn't know them after all. She doesn't know Marvin either and now he's steering her toward his cottage, which is mostly dark now.

Something is missing.

She doesn't have the backpack. Where did she leave it? Under her chair?

I need to find Fern.

The party is slowly dying down but there are still several huddled clumps of people scattered around the large property. Their voices are loud and insistent, laughing with too much exuberance or else filled with exasperation and occasional outrage. Empty bottles fall onto the lawn with hollow thunks.

She waited too long. *Fern Fern Fern Fern—*

There's a scraping sensation low in her belly until she's raw and hollow, and then Ruth doubles over and vomits onto the grass.

A few teenagers around them chuckle knowingly and Marvin bends over her, gathering strands of her hair and pulling them back. "You're not well," he says. "Let me help you."

"Fern." She wipes the drool and sick out of the corners of her sour mouth. She spits out ropes of saliva that hang there, shining.

Strong arms ease her upright, and she lets them. She's completely empty now and Fern was never inside her to begin with, but that doesn't matter, of course it doesn't matter.

"Here, rinse out your mouth." He's pressing a bottle to her lips, and she drinks. "Just a sip now, don't overdo it."

Too sweet.

"She's all right," says Marvin. Reading her mind. "I promise."

But you don't know, she wants to say. Because he's not a parent so he doesn't know anything. *That's not fair,* she scolds herself, and the scolding is a reprieve from being scared but now the fear is back and it's worse and *where is her child?*

She must be with the twins. They're off having fun somewhere.

Ruth stumbles along with Marvin and pictures a mound of sand with her daughter inside it.

189

Fern wouldn't have struggled at first because they were all playing and of course Isabelle and Amelia were going to dig her out when they were done—they were her friends! They were practically her sisters. They would've smiled as they patted the sand down around her, so smooth, and it would've been cool on her skin, and heavy. They were playing a game and Fern got to be buried first, and soon only her head was poking out and wasn't that funny, and they all laughed together, but then Isabelle or maybe Amelia would've shouted, "Let's bury *all* of you!" And Fern would've agreed because she loves them. And the people we love want to help us, not hurt us. It's the strangers we have to worry about.

"We'll have to be quiet," says Marvin. "Lesley will be sleeping."

She wants to ask how he knows that too, but of course couples just know things about each other. She and James can look at each other and know if something is wrong. They can tell just by looking. They don't even have to ask.

Now Marvin is guiding her up the creaky steps of their front porch, and Ruth frowns. So why didn't he know that she didn't want him to go away with Stef all those times? Even though he had to, for work.

Cruises and resorts and hotels, for team building, where everybody had to wear the same T-shirt with the company logo on it, and play tug-of-war and lead each other around a conference room blindfolded, and James always complained afterward that he hated all that stuff, but at least Stef was there to make it bearable.

And Ruth would laugh and say yes, it was a good thing Stef was with him.

But he left when Ruth was bleeding and he also left too soon the other time. And her father died when James was away and he should've been home but he wasn't. He was on a boat with Stef instead, getting sick on seafood salad. Rubbery clams in bad mayonnaise. That made Ruth feel a little better at least, later on.

They're inside now and Marvin closes the door behind them and holds a finger up to his lips. "Shh."

The living room is dark but she can make out the big shape of the couch and the smaller shape of the steamer trunk as they pass by. Its lovely green is dimmed now, nearly black.

Her legs are unsteady and she wobbles a bit, but Marvin braces her.

"Let's go upstairs," he says. "I want to show you something."

She's here, thinks Ruth, with absolute certainty, but she keeps the thought to herself because she needs to be stealthy. She can't let on that she knows.

Fern is with Lesley. Of course she is. It's ridiculous that Ruth is just figuring this out now. The way Lesley looked at her. She's been waiting for her opportunity, dreaming of a child of her own.

Ruth used to read other people's birth announcements about their happy, healthy, bouncy babies, and the rush of grief and resentment would surprise her every time, because she expected to be glad for them. She'd pull the little, white envelope with its sharp corners out of her mailbox, or click on the proudly trumpeting subject line, and stare numbly at the photo of someone else's beautiful newborn. She wanted to celebrate with them but she couldn't. All she could do was delete the email, or crumple up the card and take it outside and walk with it burning in her hand until she found a bin far away to bury it in.

Marvin guides her up the stairs, helping to support her weight because she's floppy and lightheaded. He makes her feel light.

I'll run in and grab her.

They reach the top and keep walking.

I'll carry her to safety.

They pass the empty guestroom, and then the empty bathroom. The hallway is so long.

We'll go home and everything will be all right again and we'll all be happy.

They pass the master bedroom, where Lesley and her doll are sound asleep on their nest of pillows.

Not there. Ruth sags against Marvin.

"So peaceful," he says. "But I can guess what she's dreaming about."

Ruth moans. A small sound that grows, and this is all she can do. Everything is wrong and she can't make it better.

"Shh." He tugs her away and they continue down the hall together, getting closer to the room at the end of it with the closed door.

It must be him, then. The one who worried her from the beginning. Why does she never listen? Because he focused on her, and she liked it.

Her mind skitters around the edges of the bad things Marvin might do to her daughter—might have already done—and she shakes her head against the images of him and Fern that rise up.

As they walk, the white walls flicker dimly with all the bad things that grown-ups do to kids every day, everywhere in the world. Little mouths screaming and grieving parents on their knees.

She tries to puzzle it out, though, and can't. He's been with Ruth the whole time. There is no way.

Her phone begins to vibrate. She reaches into her back pocket and fumbles with it, nearly drops it, but holds on.

"Here we are," Marvin says. And he opens the door.

The tiny screen lights their way. There are words on it for her and she needs to read them but they're too small and she's moving too fast.

James must be checking in again. He misses them.

Marvin pulls her inside and shuts the door with a click that's louder than the insistent buzzing.

Ruth tries to steady the phone with her shaking hand, trying to read the message but all she can see is the name blinking at her from the little window.

Stef. Not James after all. Their names are always so close together, though.

Marvin takes the phone from her, gently but firmly, and she doesn't try to take it back.

Her eyes have started to adjust, and she can discern the outlines of objects all around them. There is a large pile of small shapes against one wall.

"We forgot to take off our shoes." His voice lowers, conspiratorial. "Don't worry, though, we won't tell Lesley." And he eases her down so she's sitting somewhere soft.

She's on a bed and something is next to her, crouching on four legs. A table. *But what's on it?* A lamp, maybe. The contours are odd, though, if that's what it is. Round bumps instead of straight lines.

"I knew we'd end up here." Marvin sits down on the bed too. "As soon as I met you, I knew it."

This was a mistake, she thinks. The thought fills her fuzzy head until there's no room for anything else. *This was a mistake this was a mistake this was a mistake.*

He glances at her phone in his hand, nodding as he reads. "Stef says she found Fern, so you can stop worrying now." He holds up the tiny, helpful machine and presses a button so her friend's message glows in the dark. "See?" he says. "I told you."

Then he sets the phone down by his feet and slides it across the floor to the other end of the room, where it hums for a while longer and then is still.

Fern is safe.

"There," he says. "Now we're alone."

But Ruth is not.

"What did you put in my drink?" she asks, and the force of her voice surprises her because he is the strong one here and she is weak, and he can do anything he wants to her because now they're alone and the door is closed and how did she let this happen? *This was a mistake.*

"Nothing," he says. "It was only fruit punch. You're just very drunk and very high."

"I don't believe you."

"I can't control what you believe." He shrugs against her and the movement nearly knocks her over. "But I'm telling the truth."

Now her fear is for herself, and the last of her strength drains out with a *whoosh*. Everything inside of her is cold. Everything inside of her is looking at the door that is closed and thinking about the other side. The wide-open hallway and the stairs down to the living room with its attractive, comfortable furniture and the front door that opens onto the sweet, fresh air and the smoke from the bonfire and the people laughing and dancing and drinking, but she is in here.

It was better when she was out there. It was better when she was not in here.

I told you. I told you.

But now this is where she is.

"I would never hurt you," Marvin says quietly. "I hope that you know that."

There have been so many times in her life when she has told herself, *Don't worry, it will be fine.* And it was. There have been times when she has thought, *This is a bad idea.* And she listened. And everything was fine.

She knows that she has been lucky so far.

There have been times when she has witnessed other women walking into bad situations and she just let them go because, oh well, they knew what they were getting into. She wishes she'd said something to them now. *Don't go. Be safe and stay here with me.*

There was one time when she left a girl alone in a basement with two boys and never went back for her. She wishes she'd gone back. But she was young and scared and her friend was brave and anyway she was fine after all. "I just screamed and they let me go," Stef told Ruth when the two of them were alone later, flipping through fashion magazines on Ruth's bed, and they never talked about it again.

"Lesley spends a lot of time in this room," Marvin says, mostly to himself. "I used to come in here a lot too, but not so much anymore. Too many bad memories."

Ruth wonders how James would feel if he knew. He would've rushed to Stef's rescue, she knows that much. Would he rush to Ruth's rescue now, if he knew she was in danger? She thinks he would. Probably. But he's so far away. It would take him too long to get here, even if he drove very fast.

Once, when Ruth was very pregnant, she and James had a picnic. They went to the little park near their apartment and tried to find a nice spot to sit, but there was only dirt and dried-out patches of grass because most of the trees had been cut down by the city. They had some sort of bug in them. James said, "Oh well," and spread the lobster towel out over the greenest section, but when they sat down, they could feel everything through the thin material. Rocks and twigs and the sharp spines of discarded feathers. There was even a small, broken piece of shell that poked right into the back of her thigh, and Ruth held it up and said, "How did this get here?" James said, "A seagull must've dropped it." And they were both quiet for a long time. Ruth was thinking about how far away the lake was. She didn't know what James was thinking, which bothered her. She'd never been able to tell.

Marvin sits very still beside her, breathing in the dark. Then he shifts his weight subtly, moving against her as he lifts his hand and brings it to her face.

Ruth flinches away but not quite in time, and the stranger strokes her cheek before he reaches across her and switches on the bedside lamp.

And all at once the room is very bright, and she can see.

There is the bumpy lamp. Under the lightbulb with its striped, circus-tent shade, a laughing clown clutches a bunch of balloons in all different colours, floating on sharp-looking strings. The red paint on his mouth has worn away, as if someone used to rub it.

"It's easier to let new people think we never had children to begin with," Marvin says. "And the neighbours who knew us before don't talk about it, because it upsets them."

Ruth squints against the harsh, yellow light.

"We just have to keep this door closed. That's the hardest part."

The small shapes are stuffed animals—bears and frogs and elephants and lambs. There are so many of them and they're all smiling. She thinks she sees something familiar, a green glint, but her eyes must be playing tricks.

"His name was Alex. Lesley called him Alexander but he liked Alex better. He liked me better too"—Marvin clears his throat, making it a silly sound—"but you didn't hear that from me."

The bed is small, and covered by a quilt decorated with farm scenes. Little red barns and white fences and bales of hay and cows and horses and chickens.

"The fire is always for him," says Marvin. "Like one big birthday candle every summer."

This room faces the water. She'd caught a glimpse of it through the shifting shadows of the trees before Marvin switched on the lamp. The night is inky black outside the window, which has been placed low on the wall. Just the right height for a small child to look out at the lake.

Exactly the way we wanted it, Lesley had told her. *It's our dream come true.*

Marvin grasps Ruth's hand and gives it a squeeze. "We had to try for a long time too, like you did. But then we had Alex and he was such a good kid. Before we lost him, he was just starting to learn to swim, and one day we were in the lake together. I let go of him for just a second and he went under. When I pulled him back up, he coughed up a bunch of water but he was smiling. I told him I was sorry and he said, 'It's okay, Daddy.'" He makes a strangled sound and looks apologetic for it.

The room isn't blue and that's good, Ruth thinks. *Too many boys' rooms are blue these days, and what if the boy doesn't like blue?* The sunny yellow walls are decorated with pictures of more animals. The one closest to Ruth shows a bright-green turtle floating on bright-blue water over the words, "The tortoise drifted out to sea. It wasn't long before he was out of sight." She wonders if that's from a story. It seems like it must be.

"We used to play hide-and-seek a lot," Marvin says. "He loved that game."

A paper airplane dangles from the ceiling. A soccer ball is wedged into the bottom shelf of a bookcase.

"And then one time I couldn't find him forever. He found a really good spot."

Ruth wants to ask him where, but then she knows. Because the answer is the punchline to Fern's favourite knock-knock joke. The one Marvin liked so much.

"He was the best hider. And so quiet, so he wouldn't give himself away." Marvin is still holding her hand but his grip is tighter now. "He never even called for help, for me to let him out. He must've just fallen asleep in there." His hand constricts around hers and all of the bones are pressed together, forced to be smaller and smaller and it hurts, *it hurts*. But then he lets her go.

Ruth pulls her hand to her chest and cradles it there, her heart thudding against her throbbing fingers.

In a far corner, a red fire truck sits silently with its white rescue ladder extended and empty. So there are a few stereo-typical boy things in the room, after all. It's hard to avoid. Ruth never planned on dressing Fern in all pink and purple, but that's what she wants.

"We kept the trunk because Lesley won't let me get rid of it. It's been three years now and she won't even talk to me about him, but we still have to look at that goddamn thing every single day. It's a pretty green, at least." His sorrow is so wide. It expands inside him, breathing through him. "Once in a while we babysit someone else's kids, so Lesley can pretend. And every night I make her a cup of her special tea, so she can sleep." He pauses and looks at Ruth intently. "I promise I wasn't lying about your drink. I'm always careful with Lesley's medicine because it's very strong."

"Okay," she says, but only because he's waiting for an answer.

He nods, and continues. "Lesley keeps Alex's baby doll in our bed with her because that was his favourite toy. Like your Fern and her dragon."

Ruth remembers the look on Lesley's face when the doll tumbled down the stairs. Full of pain that Ruth hadn't understood.

Marvin gives her the smallest smile. "He was three and a half, like your Fern too. But not like her, because she's going to keep growing and growing. And one day you'll look at her and she'll be all grown up and you'll barely recognize her. She won't even look like you anymore."

Anymore, he said. She grabs onto the word and holds it tight.

"Stef told me everything," he says, gently. "I'm so sorry that happened to you."

Tears prickle at the corners of Ruth's eyes, and then her vision blurs from them. They stream out of her.

From the bedside table, beside the awful clown lamp, Marvin plucks a tissue from a box and places the white wing against Ruth's face. Dabbing it delicately wherever her skin is wet. "We always keep these in here," he says. "They do the job."

Ruth nods. Or at least she thinks she does.

"About a week after Alex was born, Lesley told me something amazing." He's looking past her now. "He was napping so she was trying to sleep too. She was in our bed and he was in a little basket we kept beside it, and a feeling came over her. She started twisting around, getting tangled in the sheets." His voice is filled with wonder and he's staring at the turtle picture. "She said she felt like she was moulting. Shedding her old skin so

199

she could grow her new mother skin." He gazes at Ruth again. "Did that ever happen to you, with Fern?"

Almost, she wants to say. *But not quite.*

She has the memory of how her first daughter felt, at least. Her bare skin on Ruth's bare skin. The way they fused together on their island of hospital bed under the fluorescent light, after they used to be one.

"You don't have to answer me," he says. "I know it's hard."

The two of them are alone here together in this little boy's room filled with lonely toys, and Ruth wants to wrap her arms around Alex's father and tell him, *Shh, it's all right,* but she doesn't. Because it's not, and she's afraid.

"But you can understand how it feels." Marvin clasps his big hands together and traps them between his knees. "I could tell that about you right away. Even if Stef hadn't told me, I would've known."

In all of her life, no one has ever given her this much attention. Not as long as Stef has been there to steal it.

No, she corrects herself. *There is someone.*

Sometimes she lies in bed next to Fern and tries to memorize every detail of her face because she knows it won't be exactly the same in the morning. Some small aspect of it will shift overnight and then her daughter will be new in a way that Ruth can't place, but she'll know something has changed. So she lies there and looks. There is the curve of her cheek, the pink swell of her lips. Her smooth forehead, the very slight point of her chin. And Ruth whispers, when Fern is asleep, "I will keep you safe." Even though she knows this is impossible.

Ruth feels the thin, invisible wire between her and Marvin quivering. It extends past them to the doorknob and tugs at her like the clown is tugging on his bunch of balloons.

"Marvin," she says, "I'd like some fresh air. Could you please open the window, just a crack?"

"Of course." He stands up and walks away to grant her wish. He eases the window open, and the woodsy tang of distant smoke immediately fills the room. The echo of faraway revellers drifts in too and then Ruth is up and running, pushing herself toward the exit because Fern is somewhere on the other side and what will she do if Ruth is gone?

"No!" Marvin shouts behind her, his voice full of desperate fury and hurt, and he's running too and now she's pulling on the doorknob and now he's wrenching her fingers off of it, yanking her back roughly with his arms around her waist.

She struggles against him but then goes limp because it will be easier that way. He tosses her onto the bed and she curls into a C shape and tries to make herself smaller and smaller until she disappears, but it doesn't work.

"I'm sorry." He's breathing hard. "I don't want you to leave yet." He sits down next to her again, heavily. "But I should've asked you politely. Please stay. Okay?"

She nods for him, the slightest upward movement of her chin.

On the middle shelf of the bookcase there is a tall glass jar full of something, it's not close enough to tell what. Coins? Rocks? She could run and grab the jar and smash it on the floor and then she'd have the shards to use. Even if they cut her, she could use them.

Marvin sees her looking. "That's our shell collection," he tells her. "Alex and I found them together. It took us a long time to fill up the jar. But we did it, in the end." Then he reaches over and turns off the light.

"Why did you do that?" she hears herself asking in a

201

voice that's too high, almost a whine. "Why did you turn off the light?"

He lies down beside her. "Because I want to tell you a story."

A sob falls out of her then and she closes her mouth tight. She presses her hands there to keep everything in. He throws an arm around her and she tries to pull away from him but he's everywhere, the heat and weight of him pressed against her. So she lies still and listens to him talk, and waits.

"Every so often our power would go out in the cottage," he says, "and Alex would get scared. We always explained that it was only temporary and that people were working hard to fix the problem. We'd make a game out of it and put candles everywhere, but he'd always hide in his bed and make Lesley or me lie with him. One night the power went out and I was lying with him and the cottage was completely dark. I couldn't sleep because it was so quiet. I could hear every little creak. Usually I sleep with the fan on, even though Lesley complains that it makes her cold. Even if I point it at the wall. But I can't sleep without the noise, so I put it on anyway. But that night there wasn't any power and I was lying right where you are. Alex was cuddled up close to me and his eyes were closed, but then they were open because there were a bunch of loud sounds outside. Rumbling, banging, slamming and men's voices. Then a flashing yellow light came on outside his window. Alex blinked and rubbed his eyes, and then he started shaking. He said a funny thing, and I said, 'Shh, don't worry, of course not.' I told him to go back to sleep and he did. Because it didn't make any sense, what he was saying. He was still half in a dream."

"What did he say?" Ruth asks in a whisper.

"He said, 'Don't let them take me away, Daddy.'" A sigh shudders out of him and he moves even closer, wrapping all of himself around her.

This time Ruth doesn't try to get away. What would be the point? He's bigger and stronger than she is, and she's tired.

"The next morning we woke up and the power was back on, like magic. Lesley made us pancakes and then she went out grocery shopping, and Alex and I stayed home and played hide-and-seek." Marvin is crying now, very softly. "I never actually looked out the window, you know. I imagined the hydro workers with their orange vests and their tools and their truck with the yellow flashing light. But I never actually saw them."

And then he's pulling at her, rolling her over, and she lets him. She allows him to move her body so she's facing him. Their heads are only inches apart on the pillow, which is damp from his tears.

His pupils are very large, she notices now. There is only the thinnest green ring surrounding the glassy black circles. Cartoon eyes.

His breath is hot and sweet but the men's room at the park had smelled so awful, she remembers that now. How did she forget the smell? The ripe, wet rot of it had filled her nose and she wanted to plug her nostrils but she couldn't because the man's face was too close to hers. Breathing on her and then his tongue was in her mouth and it was a live thing burrowing, filling her up. His teeth scraped against hers and his mouth was a clam with the shell smashed open and the slimy guts hanging out, rubbing against her lips and chin and making them slimy too. And then Stef was calling for her, setting her free.

"Ruth!"

The shout comes from outside. Below the window, which Marvin opened just a crack.

"Where are you?" Stef's voice reaches for them through the glass.

203

"I knew I should've left the light off the whole time." Marvin sighs. "But I wanted you to see."

Ruth tries to sit up, tries to call out, "I'm here!" But his heavy arm is pressing her down so she can only lie there, doing nothing.

"Ruth!" Stef is louder, getting closer. Coming to save her again.

"Is she a good friend?" Marvin asks. "I've been wondering about that."

"Ruth!" Another voice from outside, deep and booming. "Are you in there?" Sammy is looking for her too. That's nice of him.

"I'm going to go now," Marvin says. "But I need to tell you a secret first. It's only for you, because no one else wants to listen."

"*What are you going to give me for it?*" said the stranger in the tiki bar. He was joking at first but then he wasn't.

Marvin's nose is touching hers and his tears are on her cheeks. "I miss him."

And then he kissed her. Mashed his mouth against hers and she squeezed her eyes shut tight, and he walked her backwards until her back was pressed against the wall and all around them everyone was dancing and laughing and nobody cared. They stood under the flamingo while the rainbow-coloured disco ball turned and turned and made everything beautiful, and her husband was far away with someone else and he didn't care either.

"Auntie Ruth!" More voices now. A chorus of them, coming to find her.

Then she went home alone and turned on all the lights in their quiet apartment, and she stuck a new maxi-pad into her underwear and threw out the old one and got into bed, and she was too tired to change out of her tight clothes but she still didn't fall asleep for a very long time.

"I miss him," Marvin says again, more urgently this time, but so quietly that only Ruth can hear. "I miss my Alex so much."

She doesn't turn away. She doesn't close her eyes. She lies there and listens and lets him cry, and waits.

The front door bangs open and closed downstairs. The noise is softened by Alex's door, shut tight against the rest of the world.

She pictures a boy curled up in his dark hiding spot, smiling because his daddy couldn't find him, and then closing his eyes and drifting off to sleep. Almost the same as what happened to her own baby, who'd been snug and safe inside Ruth for the longest time, until something went wrong.

"Mama!"

That one word reaches her, above all the other sounds.

Marvin smiles a little and finally pulls away. "There she is."

He takes another tissue from the box and carefully dries her face, but not his own. "Life keeps going." He leans in again. There's a new looseness to his mouth, and his voice is slightly slurred when he whispers, "But I'm not prepared." Then he stands up and goes to the door and opens it. "Thank you, Ruth."

And then he's gone. And Ruth is alone with the tortoise on the wall, both of them drifting out to sea.

Footsteps pound down the hall, getting closer. Big and little. Little and big.

"Ruth!"

"Mama!"

And then she appears. The one she was waiting for all along.

Fern runs over to the bed and lays her head on Ruth's belly. "Mama, why are you sleeping?"

"I'm not sleeping, honey." Ruth smiles at her. Marvelling at her. Relief is flooding all of her limbs and she's buzzing with it. "I'm awake."

And then her friend is there. Silhouetted in the dark doorway for a moment before she runs in too, but her familiar face is less familiar now. Because Stef never worries about anything.

"Marvin just ran past us and said you'd be fine. At least I think that's what he said. He's pretty wasted. What the hell was he talking about?" Stef gazes around the room then, her eyes wide. "Holy shit."

"We did sparklers!" says Fern. "And we threw our marshmallows into the fire and they exploded! But I ate some too. They tasted like clouds, I think. And the fire was hot but I didn't let it get me. Then we went to Marvin's beach but Auntie Stef found us and said we weren't being safe. We were playing too close to the water and the water isn't safe at night."

The twins barrel in then, followed by Sammy.

He leans against the door frame, huffing and puffing. Then he gapes around the room too, taking everything in. "Wait a minute. Holy shit. I thought they didn't have kids."

"They don't." Ruth strokes Fern's hair. "But they did."

She is about to tell them that his name was Alex, but she keeps that detail to herself. It wouldn't help anyone if they knew it anyway.

Stef walks over and sits next to her, and heaves the backpack onto the bed between them. "We were looking for you and I saw this under your chair and I was like, *When does she ever leave* that *behind?* And then I texted you about Fern and you didn't text me back, which was even weirder. That's when I started freaking out."

Isabelle and Amelia are examining Alex's toys now, holding them up and turning them this way and that, and Fern wanders over to join them.

Ruth sits up and pulls the backpack onto her lap. She looks at Stef. "I'm glad you're here."

"Mama!" Fern calls, holding something up. "I found your phone!"

"Thanks, honey," says Ruth. "I don't need it now."

Stef looks at the phone, so far away from them, and back to Ruth. "How—"

Ruth shakes her head.

"Why do Marvin and Lesley have all this little-kid stuff?" says Isabelle. "It's dumb for adults to have this stuff."

"I thought he was harmless." Stef reaches out a shaky hand to smooth some hair out of Ruth's eyes.

Ruth had wanted to do that for her too once, when Stef was lying on the hospital bed and Ruth was holding Fern, and James was standing beside them with the biggest smile.

After Fern was born she let out the loudest wail, and Ruth and James cried too. She was a mother now and he was a father, and what a wonder that was. And their baby was crying so much and whoever knew that could be such a good sound, and they leaned against each other and wept with her, marvelled at her. The miraculous reality of her. Here was their daughter, who had finally stayed.

Ruth had wanted to place her cool hand against her friend's shining brow and push the damp hair away so Stef could see all of their gratitude. How big it was.

But then Stef grinned around the room, taking everyone

207

in, and when she had the attention of the smiling doctor and nurses and medical students and James, always James, she said, "Okay, who's next? Stitch me up and get me some Gatorade and I'm good to go."

And they all laughed and laughed, and then Ruth joined in too. But her hand stayed on Fern, holding her tight.

"Nothing happened," says Ruth. "He just wanted to talk to me."

Stef pinches one of the zippers on the backpack and tugs it open and closed, open and closed. "You're lucky, then."

Ruth hears the hardness in her friend's voice, but then her own voice goes flat. "Marvin said you told him everything."

"But I didn't." Stef shakes her head, frowning. "I only told him about the end. I know you don't like to talk about the beginning."

The night is warm and close, and the room smells like smoke. Sammy stands by the window looking out, and the two mothers watch their children play.

"Actually," Ruth says slowly, "I don't like to talk about any of it."

"Yes, because that's the healthiest way to do things, isn't it?"

Ruth tugs at the quilt, wanting to pull it over her, but it's stuck beneath them. "It didn't happen to you."

"You're right." Stef nods. "Other stuff happened to me instead."

Sammy looks over at them, his eyes darkening. He raises an eyebrow at Stef, but she gives him the tiniest swivel of her head, and Ruth tries to remember exchanging just one unspoken signal like this with James, but she comes up empty.

All three girls have turned toward them now too, bright blonde heads tilted attentively.

"What's wrong, Mama?" Fern asks.

"Careful," Stef murmurs, so only Ruth can hear. "Little ears."

The two grown women are squashed together on the little bed. Ruth can feel the heat of her friend's thigh pressed against hers. "Nothing's wrong, honey."

"I'm just glad you're all right." Stef is still holding the zipper tightly, her forearm pushing down on Ruth's knee. "I'm glad he didn't hurt you."

Somewhere in the middle of the long, silent car ride back to Ruth's parents' house, away from the boys and their blanket and the sad hero on TV, Stef had started crying. Ruth's dad asked if she was okay and she didn't answer, she just cried harder, so he asked Ruth the same question. "Is Stef okay?" But Ruth didn't say a word.

"I was going to come down and get you when he got there," Ruth whispers to her friend now, in this small room. "I wasn't going to just leave."

Stef is focusing all of her attention on the backpack, refusing to meet Ruth's gaze, but her hands aren't moving anymore. They're completely still. "I know you weren't."

The inside of Ruth's mouth is still tacky with sugar, the sharp aftertaste of Marvin's fruit punch lingering on her tongue and teeth. She swallows but it won't go away.

She and Stef sit there while their lies float up, knotted together. Drifting over their daughters and out the window, and then they're gone.

"I'm sorry," Ruth says, even though it doesn't matter now because it's been a million years. And then, hesitantly, "Are you okay?"

"Don't worry about me," Stef says, and finally looks up. "I'll be fine."

Ruth opens her mouth to say the other words too. She needs to say them because she hasn't yet, even after all this time. Sometimes when she's alone and she thinks about it, she'll convince herself that she must've said them already, surely. But she knows she hasn't. Not out loud. "Thank you, Stef."

Her friend doesn't move. She stays exactly where she is. "Don't mention it," she says. And smiles.

They have known each other for so long.

"There he is," Sammy says. "And there he goes."

Ruth looks over. "Who?"

"Marvin." Sammy glances back at the hallway, furrowing his brow. "When he ran past me before, he said he was done with the party and he was going to the beach. I said, 'You're going boarding *now*?' Because he sounded hammered. I told him he was being a bad host but he wasn't listening. He just pushed me out of the way and kept going. Was he *crying*?"

Ruth shakes her head. "He shouldn't do that."

"We live in a modern world, Ruth," Sammy wisecracks. "Men are allowed to cry."

"No—" And then, finally, she understands.

Suddenly Fern gasps. "There you are, you naughty boy! What were you doing, hiding up here without me?"

Ruth stands up. "You have to go after him," she tells Sammy. "Don't let him go."

"Fern," says Stef, "who are you talking to?"

Sammy's grin falters. "Why?"

"Him!" Fern yanks Monsieur Foomay out from the pile of Alex's stuffed animals and brandishes him triumphantly. "We came in here when Lesley was downstairs but nobody found us so I got bored and found the baby doll."

Ruth inhales. The same never-ending breath in that a sad

or furious child takes before the blaring wail their parents know will come. And at last, after all this time, the scream that has been buried way deep down, where no one could ever find it, starting out so tiny and weak but growing more powerful every second, uncurls and rips out of her. "*Go!*" she yells at Sammy.

His smile disappears entirely then, and he races out of the room.

"You're right." Stef stands up too. "Marvin shouldn't be out there. What the hell was he thinking?"

Ruth looks at the night on the other side of the glass. *Nothing. That's all he ever thinks about.* But she keeps that to herself.

Isabelle and Amelia and Fern hurry over to the window. They all clamber to see outside, jostling each other for the best possible view.

"I see him!" Isabelle hops up and down, holding onto the windowsill.

The twins and Fern huddle together, watching. Their arms snake around each other, and Ruth can't tell where they begin or where they end.

"I'm going too," she tells Stef, even though she knows it's too late. She knows he's already gone. "Can you stay here with the kids?"

Her friend nods.

"Bye, Marvin!" shouts Amelia.

Ruth rushes to the doorway. "Is he wearing his headlamp?"

No one answers her, and the thin wire between them stretches as far as it will go, and snaps.

"No, Marvin." Fern is shaking her head slowly. Back and forth, back and forth. "That is not a very good idea."

NINE

THE MOTHER-TO-BE HAS A SITCOM LABOUR.

There she is with her big, unwieldy belly in the grocery store, shopping for bread or milk or ground beef or something, and her water breaks all over the floor with a dramatic yet hilarious *whoosh*.

And here comes the embarrassed, pimply stock boy rushing at the oozing puddle with a mop, and here is the concerned older-lady cashier who takes her arm and says, "Should we call your husband, dear?"

And twenty minutes later, there is their car screeching into the parking lot and now the father-to-be is in the store already, and how the hell did he move so fast like that, he's like Superman, and now he's bundling the mother-to-be into the passenger seat and apologizing to her over and over and she says, "What? What are you sorry for?" And he says, "I couldn't find the overnight bag, I just couldn't find it, so I packed a new one. I'm not sure if I packed the right stuff but I think it has everything you'll need but if something is missing I'll just go back and get it for you, okay?"

The mother-to-be is already extremely annoyed with the father-to-be, way more annoyed than she expected she would feel at this early stage. Aren't they supposed to be suffused with love right now, or at least until she's fully dilated and starting transition and she catches a whiff of his peppermint gum and it smells like puke and she screams at him, "Put. That. Fucking. Gum. In. The. Garbage. Right. Fucking. Now." Which would be okay, that would be understandable, to be irritated by one's spouse at that point, but this early in the game? To be so filled with fury and with all of it directed solely at him, her beloved life partner, *while he's driving her and their unborn child to the hospital*? This does not bode well for her cherished goal of being a united front when it comes to parenthood. But whatever.

Now the father-to-be is parking their car in a no-parking zone and half carrying the mother-to-be through the sliding doors and now he's hollering her name at the triage nurse, and now the mother-to-be is in a wheelchair and the father-to-be is pushing her down the hall, frantically listing all of the baby names they've been arguing about over the past nine months, but none of them sound right.

He's running and they're going too fast, but hey, if her cervix wasn't on fire right now it would actually be kind of fun—*wheee!*

And now she's on a bed and the nurse is here, and the nurse sticks her hand into the mother-to-be's vagina and then the nurse goes to get the doctor, and now the doctor is here and she is sticking her hand into the mother-to-be's vagina as well, and soon untold medical professionals have inserted their hands or other implements into that same area that was once private but is now very, very public.

But that's okay because she's lying on the hospital bed in the delivery room, listening to nurses and doctors murmuring and the reassuring clicks and beeps of helpful machines.

It's the middle of the day and the lights are very bright and the sheets are very blue and the room smells red, and she is holding her husband's hand.

She's where she is supposed to be.

Except now all the professionals are whispering to each other differently, urgently, and the father-to-be is saying, "What's wrong? Is something wrong?"

And nobody answers him at first because now the nurse is rushing to attach the mother-to-be to something, and she hears herself asking, "Is that a fetal heart monitor?"

And the nurse nods and tells her it's okay, this is the normal procedure when there's meconium, and the father-to-be says, "Is that when the baby poops inside the womb?"

And the mother-to-be is so proud of him because clearly he was actually paying attention in their prenatal classes instead of thinking about work like she always figured he was doing.

More bad things happen and the mother-to-be doesn't feel like she's in a sitcom anymore. The baby does not want to come out on her own. The mother-to-be has been pushing and pushing, but apparently not in a useful way. And since neither of them are co-operating and doing what they're supposed to do, the doctor says, "We're going to have to use the vacuum, is that okay?" And the mother-to-be says, "Do I have a choice?" And the doctor says, "No."

So they use the vacuum and there is no time for an anaesthetic so there is *pain, pain, pain*, and the mother-to-be is so scared but when she realizes that her fear is not for herself, she becomes stronger.

She is exhausted but she pushes harder anyway. Too hard. And then, after more pain that goes on forever and ever until it rips her apart, there she is.

The Long-Sought-After Daughter. Separate at last from the mother's body, held aloft by the doctor with her bloody latex gloves, and the whole thing is very anticlimactic because the room is completely silent and the Long-Sought-After Daughter is not moving or making any noise at all, and she is blue instead of pink.

There are more furtive murmurs and suddenly the room is buzzing with activity as the doctor cuts the umbilical cord and gives the baby to a nurse, who takes her away and wraps her in a blanket and lays her on a table near more helpful machines.

The placenta comes out and the doctor catches it. Everyone is doing their job and working together and it's all very interesting to watch but there is still no crying, and the mother remembers the enthusiastic, white-haired prenatal-class teacher telling all the anxious parents-to-be that if their baby did not cry immediately after he or she was born, then they should count to ten because in that time, a healthy baby was guaranteed to cry. "Let's all try it together now!" the teacher had rallied them in her upbeat, chirpy voice. And all the expectant couples had sat there on their uncomfortable chairs with their Styrofoam cups of stale coffee and counted to ten together, slowly. And at the end of it, the teacher clapped her hands and said, "Now, that felt like a long time, didn't it?" Stunned, fearful nods all around. "But in the grand scheme of things, it's really no time at all."

In the delivery room, the mother fixes her gaze on her silent daughter and wills her to part her tiny lips and let out the wail she knows will come.

Now the father's hand is squeezing hers and his mouth is moving along with hers—

One.

—but no sound is coming from either of them because they do not want to miss it because it's going to happen any second now.

The PA system crackles to life then, startling them, and a disembodied voice says something the mother doesn't understand, but clearly other people do because the room immediately fills with more hospital staff, all of them crowding around the quiet baby and doing whatever it is they're supposed to do.

Two.

(Her friend's children are almost two years old now. Isn't that strange, how they just keep growing?)

Cry for us, please.

Three.

Her mother-in-law knitted a little outfit and her father-in-law bought balloons at the gift shop. Earlier on, the father told the mother about his parents' funny fight in the waiting room where his mom said to his dad, "What if those balloons pop and make a loud noise and scare the baby? And what if she chokes on the broken balloon skin?" Which of course would never happen, that was ridiculous.

Four.

Her own parents are out there too. Her mom brought an old, worn blanket that she'd wrapped the mother in when she was very small. It was pale yellow and trimmed with ribbon that was ragged in places but still very soft. And her dad brought the same book of fairy tales he used to read to her when she was little. They would cuddle together on her bed and their heads would be touching and she'd feel the vibrations of his deep voice through her entire body and know that she was safe.

The doctor is looking over at the nurse who took the baby away, and that nurse is shaking her head.

Please stay.

The father's parents want to be called Nanna and Poppy, and the mother's parents want to be called Grandma and Grandpa. They all agreed on that months ago.

Five.

The nurse is walking over with the baby now, but before she arrives, someone new appears beside the mother—"the specialist," she hears another nurse say. He looms over the bed in short-sleeved scrubs with his hairy arms poised and says to the mother, "We need to get you stitched up." She looks past him to her daughter and imagines how big that needle must be, to be able to put her back together after this.

"Not yet," the doctor tells the specialist. "Give her a minute."

He nods and backs away, retreating with his sewing kit to a distant corner of the room.

The doctor's kind eyes are shining over her surgical mask, which is blue like the sheets but a darker shade than the baby, and her hidden mouth asks, very gently, "Would you like to hold her?"

Six.

The mother feels herself nod. She extends her arms and accepts the limp, nearly weightless body, and lays it across her own.

"Does she have a name?" the doctor asks.

Don't go. Be safe and stay here with me.

"No." The mother shakes her head. "We couldn't think of the right one."

Her baby's eyes are closed and her black lashes fan out, impossibly long. The mother rubs one of her daughter's damp, dark curls between her thumb and her finger.

"Hello," she says, but only in her head. The way she used to say things when her daughter was still inside and it was just the two of them.

Seven.

The mother's breasts are already swollen and aching and where will all the milk go now, with no one to feed? She will never be a fountain.

The father leans closer, bowing his head against hers. "I told you," he says, so quietly that only the mother can hear.

Eight.

So it's easy to pretend that she doesn't. Even though she knows he's right.

Nine.

She holds one of the tiny hands against her cheek and it doesn't move, but she doesn't care.

James is sobbing now and he's never going to stop, so Ruth has to finish counting all by herself.

TEN

H<small>ERE SHE IS, ALONE ON THE BEACH WITH HER ONLY</small>
child. It's early in the day, and the sun is already so bright.

Stef and Sammy went out in their boat. They're out there now with the local police and the volunteer firefighters and most of their neighbours, still searching.

They left Isabelle and Amelia with Lesley because they know she'll take good care of them. And the twins will cheer Lesley up too. They'll make her feel better, at least for a little while. Even though she wasn't sad when Stef told her about Marvin, in the gentlest voice Ruth has ever heard her use. Lesley just held on to Alex's baby doll and nodded slowly, as if she was expecting this, and looked out the window. But maybe she was searching too, in her own way.

After Ruth woke up early this morning, tucked into her own guest bed safe and sound with Fern still sleeping peacefully in the next room, she called James to say they were coming home.

"Already?" he asked, and when she didn't answer, he said he was sorry he'd missed all the fun, but he promised everything would be perfect when they arrived.

"That's okay," she told him. "It wasn't that much fun after all."

And he started to say something else, something about Stef, probably, and how Ruth shouldn't be so negative about their friend who hadn't been as lucky as they were. But she didn't want to hear it, so she said goodbye and hung up.

Then she went and kissed their daughter awake, and they had breakfast with Stef and the twins before they all went to Lesley and Marvin's cottage, together but separate. Ruth drove behind Stef, their procession small and slow.

Now Ruth holds Fern's hand and squints at the sparkling water. Far off, she sees some land. Rocks, an outcropping of green. Maybe Marvin is out there on his own little island. Taking a vacation before he makes his way back home. It's a nice thought, so she holds onto it and pushes the other thoughts away.

"Can we go swimming now, Mama?"

That had been the plan—one more swim before they go— but the waves are so much bigger today.

"I don't know if we should, honey."

"But it's so hot, and we're wearing our bathing suits!"

"It might not be safe, though. And I packed your floaty in the car."

Fern's shoulders sag. "I miss Daddy."

The sky is a shocking blue, not a cloud in sight, and the glare is blinding.

"I know you do," says Ruth. "But it's good to miss people. It's good to be apart from each other sometimes because then we can see how we really feel."

They're both quiet for a while, and then Fern becomes restless beside Ruth, shifting from foot to foot. "Mama?"

"Yes, honey?"

Fern lets go of her and sits down on the sand. She moves her hands around, making patterns. "Why do you hate Auntie Stef?"

"No." Ruth lets out a breath. "I don't hate her. I could never hate her."

Fern keeps her eyes on the ground. Her hands fan out around her, drawing elaborate designs. Surrounding herself with curlicues and swirls and zigzags. "Because of me?"

"Yes, that's right." Ruth kneels next to her. "Because of you."

"But why didn't she keep me?"

"What do you mean?" Her head is foggy and sore, skewered with hangover, and she shakes it to bring her daughter's hazy form into focus. "Because you're mine."

"Because she already had Amelia and Isabelle?"

223

"No, Fern." Ruth swipes a hand roughly at the corners of her eyes, then places her palms down on the sand. "Auntie Stef had you for me, and Daddy. You were always going to be ours. We told you this."

"You didn't." Fern is finally looking at her now.

There is something so familiar about her little face, something Ruth sees in the mirror when she really looks at herself. The crease in her brow when she's confused or annoyed. Three little lines. Why didn't she notice it before?

"Daddy told you," Ruth murmurs. "I didn't. You're right."

"You never did."

Ruth had lain very still in her and James's bed that long-ago night, listening to his faraway voice on the monitor telling their daughter that she was a gift from Auntie Stef, who had grown Fern in her tummy until she was ready to meet Mommy and Daddy. She was the best present that Mommy and Daddy had ever been given, and they were so grateful.

Ruth had pulled the blanket up, securing it around her neck the way she'd done when she was a kid, so only her face poked out. Less surface area for the monsters that way. She had waited for Fern to ask him what was wrong with Mommy's tummy? Why couldn't she grow in there? But she didn't. She just said, "Okay," and went to sleep. Ruth curled up under the covers and listened to James easing himself off of Fern's bed and stepping quietly out of her room and closing the door. He stayed at the other end of the apartment and Ruth stayed in bed, and after a while she fell asleep too.

In the morning, the truth was there, but Fern just smiled at her parents and ate her cereal. So Ruth never talked about it at all.

The sun warms her shoulders. It radiates all over, filling her with light and heat. Loosening her limbs and making it easy to sit down next to her daughter and look right at her, and say in a clear and steady voice, "I'm sorry."

Fern nods. She studies a pink pebble, turning it around and around until she spots some imperfection and then flings it away.

At the cottage with her parents, Ruth would spend hours examining rocks on the beach. Admiring their smoothness and colour and degrees of shininess. She always wondered where they'd all come from. How did they end up there, with her?

Her daughter is silent for what feels like a long time, digging in the sand again. Then she stops and leans against Ruth and says, "It's okay, Mama."

Ruth leans in too, collapsing around her. She says something that sounds like, "Thank you," but it's just a noise, the feeling instead of the words, and then Fern is showing her something, holding up the amber shard proudly and waving it in the air. "Look! Treasure!"

The piece of Ruth's broken beer bottle gleams. The one piece Marvin didn't find, and he tried so hard.

"It's pretty, sweetie, but you should put it down. I don't want it to cut you."

Fern listens to her, and then her lower lip wobbles. "Pick me up."

"Okay," says Ruth, and all of the movements are so practised and familiar that she's barely aware of them as they happen, but she tries to pay attention now: knees bending, hands gripping, knees straightening, biceps flexing, hip jutting out. Then her whole body relaxes as the small arms and legs wrap around her.

She pictures a baby girl curled up in her dark hiding spot, smiling, and then closing her eyes and drifting off to sleep.

We would've given you a name, thinks Ruth. *We couldn't think of the right one, but we would've thought of it eventually.*

They stand there together by the emerald lake, under the clear blue sky and the wild, yellow sun. In the distance, toy boats patrol the horizon, trying to do something good.

"I saw him, Mama," Fern whispers, close to her ear. "I saw him go into the water like the Bog Princess."

Some neighbours had found Marvin's paddleboard in the morning, washed up on the shore by their dock.

"Was he wearing a life jacket?" Ruth asks. Hope edging into her voice.

"No." Fern shakes her head, slowly. "He was not being safe."

A shadow flies over them, and then there are more. The gulls are frenzied, fighting over something, and the air fills with their screaming before the flock breaks apart and soars away.

Marvin had disappeared by the time Sammy reached the shore. When Ruth got there a few minutes later, hopelessly out of breath, Sammy told her to tell Stef that he'd spend the night on Marvin and Lesley's couch. A few of the partygoers had arrived by boat, so he was staying behind with some of those guests to go out looking on the water.

225

Ruth only vaguely remembers the bumpy car ride back to Stef and Sammy's cottage, all of them silent with the night pressed against the windows and the dark forest reaching for them.

Lesley was deep in her drugged sleep, impossible to wake, so Stef had found the keys to Marvin and Lesley's car and drove Ruth and kids home, slowly and very carefully. Ruth sat in the back with Fern on her lap and the twins sitting on either side of her, and none of them were strapped in. Their seat belts dangled uselessly, far away from their buckles. There was no one else on the road. "We'll bring the car back in the morning," Stef said, mostly to herself. "We'll see everybody in the morning."

Ruth dimly remembers Stef parking and the car doors opening and closing, the two families walking together across the lawn and up the steps and into the cottage and then going their separate ways without a word. Ruth went downstairs with Fern and tucked her in, and they both fell asleep in their own beds.

She doesn't remember what she dreamed about.

But she remembers a moment. After she and James came home alone from the hospital.

James had called Stef on the way, and she was waiting on the steps outside their apartment. She stood up when she saw them, and her eyes were so sad.

And Ruth went to her. She walked into her friend's arms, and they were warm and strong when they wrapped around her.

"It's all right," Stef whispered to Ruth, even though she knew it wasn't. But it was the right thing to say.

James stood next to them awkwardly for a minute or so, holding the overnight bag that they hadn't needed, and then he went inside.

The sun was shining and the day was hot and it was just the two of them, like it had always been. Holding on to each other while the birds sang around them, and it was really good.

And then it wasn't. But there were moments.

And there is Fern.

"Marvin was so sad," she tells Ruth in a reverent hush, a secret she's finally confiding. "I wanted to invite him to my birthday party. He could have some cake and we wouldn't have any squishy pie."

Ruth sighs and reaches up to stroke her daughter's soft, yellow hair. "Who else would you like to invite?"

"All of my friends."

Ruth smiles. "That sounds good."

"And all the kids in my class."

"That's a lot of kids, honey. And you might not like them all."

"Nope," says Fern. "I will."

"Okay, we'll see." Her daughter is getting heavy, but Ruth keeps holding her tightly. "How do you feel about school starting? Are you worried about it?"

"I don't get worried. I want my cake to be vanilla cupcakes with sprinkles."

Ruth laughs. "Noted."

Fern starts counting with her fingers. "We have to invite Nanna and Poppy and Grandma."

Ruth's smile wavers, but she nods anyway. And sends some extra love to her dad, who would've been such a wonderful grandpa.

"And Daddy and Auntie Stef and Uncle Sammy and Amelia and Isabelle."

"Of course. They'll always be invited." Ruth pauses, listening to the silence she's made. It's full of distance and absence and relief. And a closeness that's been right in front of her all this time, waiting. (*Knock, knock.*) "No matter what."

Fern looks at her. "And you, Mama. I want you there the most."

"Oh." The word falls out of her, and she doesn't trust herself to say anything else yet so she just kisses Fern on the cheek and stays there for a moment.

Her daughter's skin is impossibly soft, and sticky from something. And her breath is sweet, probably from some illicit frosted breakfast treat that Stef let her have on the sly.

228

It doesn't matter.

She blinks back the tears because she won't let them come. Not yet. She takes a shaky breath and says, "I'm looking forward to it."

"Can we please go swimming now?" Fern asks again.

Ruth bends down and lets go of her daughter, and this time she says yes.

"Yes!" Fern echoes.

The two of them stand beside each other, one little and one big. The trees are filled with singing birds behind them and the lake is wide open in front of them.

Then Fern reaches up and grabs her hand, and Ruth holds on as they walk to the water together.

And when they're almost there, they start to run.

ACKNOWLEDGEMENTS

I'M GRATEFUL FOR THE FINANCIAL SUPPORT I RECEIVED for *Worry* from the Ontario Arts Council through their Recommender Grants for Writers program (and thank you to the publishers who recommended my work).

My heartfelt thanks:

To all of the readers, librarians and booksellers (with an extra shout-out to the phenomenal independent bookstore folks).

To my exceptional editor Jennifer Lambert, for your invaluable suggestions, super-precise edits and staggering insight. From our very first meeting and throughout the entire process, you've connected with this story and helped me to clarify exactly what I wanted it to do, and then got me there. Thank you for the tremendous care you've taken with *Worry*. It's been such a joy to work with you.

To Patrick Crean for seeing a spark in an early draft of *Worry*, for our coffee meetings that buoyed me up and for guiding me from chamber music to the symphony.

To Karmen Wells for her notes on *Worry* that made me grin wildly, to Suzanne Sutherland for her excitement from the start and to Iris Tupholme, Lisa Rundle, Michael Guy-Haddock and the rest of the incredible HarperCollins Canada team for their dedication and their wonderfully warm welcome. I'm grateful for Catherine Dorton's copy-editing wizardry, Jess Shulman's meticulous proofreading, Natalie Meditsky's stellar production editing and Jaclyn Hodsdon's dazzling publicity work. For gorgeous typesetting and the perfect cover, many thanks to Alan Jones.

To Sam Hiyate for helping me develop this story, for giddy texts back and forth and for being in my writing corner from the very beginning.

To my dear first readers. Without their ongoing encouragement and brilliant feedback, I never would've figured this book out. A bazillion thanks to: Shannon Alberta for our magical phone chats and for energizing me the whole way along; Teri Vlassopoulos for sharing my glee and for early motivation at a sunny picnic; Sara Heinonen for uncanny perception up above the city and in the garden; Grace O'Connell (lit-wife extraordinaire) for shedding light early on at a candlelit Bellwoods Brewery; Kelli Deeth for Thursday-night insight over beers at our spot; Ali Lamontagne for her marvellous art and for being my fellow Fool; Robin Spano for uplifting literary gab sessions and belly laughs; Jim Munroe (Hoity King) for many years of thoughtful critique and sage advice at Buddha's; Neil Smith for wisdom and boundless championing.

To Val Quann for her excited reading and encouragement.

To Dharini Woollcombe for her generous reading and support.

To Meg Wolitzer for stick figures at brunch, inspiration at the Ritz-Carlton and for helping to make my outline sound like something out of *The New York Times*.

To Zoe Whittall for her moving endorsement and her wonderful writing.

To Ann Ireland for seeing the teacher in me and for "no fiddle-faddle."

To Kelvin Kong for early encouragement and legendary Lahore Tikka House pilgrimages.

To the Salonists for brilliance and guidance and friendship. Special thanks to Maria Meindl and Elizabeth Ruth.

To Conan Tobias, who published an early excerpt of *Worry* in *Taddle Creek*, and who has been cheering on my writing since the days of "Steak and Eggs."

To Andrew Pyper and Elisabeth de Mariaffi, whose beautifully spooky novels inspired me to write my own version of a scary story.

To the editors who heartened me with the interest they showed early on, especially Kiara Kent, Jen Knoch, Bryan Ibeas and Hermione Thompson. And to Scott Fraser for the most amazing reader's report that was instrumental in helping me fix a lot of what was wrong.

To Jen Noble for falling down with me in alleyways after long-ago spicy falafels, and for sharing elation and dejection throughout.

To Jasmine Macaulay for cheese Danishes during Psychology and Oja after the Varsity, and for being there for the highs and lows. And many thanks to Dr. Viren Naik for the medical fact-checking.

To Steve Sakamoto for never giving up on my long-abandoned high-school sci-fi tale about world-weary cowboys tasked with wrangling ornery lab-grown meat.

To Brittan Ullrich for saving me with her nursing knowledge, and for that breathless talk about plot over mini-pizzas.

To Karen Becker for reassuring advice and celebratory tea.

To Amy Silverman for morale-boosting and popcorn.

To Sheryl Faith for her eleventh-hour rescue.

To Kate and Nousheen, dearest freighbours.

To (Aunt) Betty Dick, for cheering me on since I was a baby with a bottlecap on my head.

To my cousin (Auntie) Kate Barton, for (among so much else) an excellent talk on an airplane with a much-needed tiny bottle of wine.

To my cousin Don McKellar: rinkrat, international explorer and champion pick-up-sticker.

To (Great) Aunt Lori for her love and support and strength.

To Grandma (Great G-G) Marion for being famous in McDonald's, for all that she's taught me and for endless love.

To Klaus (Opa) Wuenschirs, Jane (Yia-Yia) Wuenschirs and (Uncle) Jason Wuenschirs for all of their love and support.

To (Uncle) Cameron Westhead and (Aunt) Marcella Campbell for all of their love and for cheerleading with the kitties.

To my dad, Tim (Poppa) Westhead, for showing me the stars (above us and onscreen). To my mom, Linda (Grandma) Westhead, for always waiting for me to end our hugs first. To both of you, for always believing in me.

To Derek Wuenschirs for being with me through all of it, for consoling me and whooping with me, for never grumbling when I woke you up scribbling by flashlight in the middle of the night, for making me laugh, helping me be a better human and being the other half of the united parenting front I always dreamed of. I love you.

And to Luisa. For writing and reading with me, for being so patient when I disappeared into this story all the time, for fortune tellers and Crazy Eggs on the GO Train and other adventures, for making me laugh, helping me be a better human and always reminding the three of us to jump up and down on hotel beds. I love you. XOXO